BESIDE THE STILL WATERS

Beside the Still Waters

a novel
by

P. DAVID HORNIK

BOOKS

Adelaide Books
New York / Lisbon
2019

BESIDE THE STILL WATERS
A novel
By P. David Hornik

Published by Adelaide Books, New York / Lisbon
adelaidebooks.org

Editor-in-Chief
Stevan V. Nikolic

For any information, please address Adelaide Books
at info@adelaidebooks.org

or write to:

Adelaide Books
244 Fifth Ave. Suite D27
New York, NY, 10001

ISBN-10: 1-950437-62-0
ISBN-13: 978-1-950437-62-7

Printed in the United States of America

to Sarah, Yonatan, and Itamar

Contents

to Tami

"And she lets the river answer that you've

always been her lover...."

Leonard Cohen,
"Suzanne"

Preface

by Steve Sandorsky

A few words about this book and how it came to be.

I've never particularly been involved with the genre of autobiography. I've read a few autobiographies here and there, but I didn't seek out books in that category. Recently, though, as part of my work as a translator from Hebrew to English, an autobiography came my way for translating, and when you translate a book, you get very intimately involved with it. This book—written by a person who is almost the same age as I am—intrigued me in a more personal way, until I realized that what the author had done, I too wanted to do: tell my own story.

My way of telling it, though, turned out to be unconventional in the sense that it's not a linear, year-by-year account. Maybe I didn't have the patience for that, or maybe I saw my story as best represented by a series of focal points or episodes—several of which were crises. This is, then, an episodic kind of autobiography. It skips over spans of years, landing on focal points, but still it aims to give a more or less full view of how things developed.

And finally, the story ends quite a few years before the time in which these lines are being written. For one thing, as you get closer to the present, issues of privacy come to the fore, and it gets harder to write about people without giving away too much about them. But also, a big effort was being made to tie things together, to take the different pieces of a mess and gather them into a whole.

Steve Sandorsky
Tel Aviv, 2019

Beginnings, 1958-1966

1

In 1958 my family moved northward from New York City to Renford Park, which is near Schenectady. I was four years old and my sister Nellie was three. My parents—Arnold and Tricia (Ainslee) Sandorsky—chose a small, one-story brick house, set back from the road in a lush yard, and there Nellie and I grew up, and there my parents lived until my father died in 1978 and, a few years later, my mother moved elsewhere.

From such a distance in time as well as space, much of the memory of those days is now pastoral and idyllic. In our backyard there was a line of silver maples and firs, and beyond that was a farther reach of the backyard, bounded only by woods. It was in that farther reach of the backyard that my parents, after we'd lived there two or three years, had a large aboveground pool installed. It had a mahogany deck from which, in summer mornings, Nellie and I jumped blissfully into the bright, bouncing water. I had a toy water-polo set, with a hoop attached by metal rods to an inflatable stand, a small, basketball-like ball; it was all I needed for breathless, splashing fantasy-matches between teams I made up.

Our house was at a junction; to its right was Renford Park Center Road, and straight ahead was Kaisley Road, across which was the cornfield of a farm. I was there some years ago, and the cornfield, the farm, are gone now, replaced by a strip mall. But in those days the cornfield was always a serene place for the eyes to rest. Renford Park was still—except for the town itself and some developments—very rural; it was farm country that except for some cars and telephone lines might not have changed since the time of a much older America.

If you followed Renford Park Center Road about a mile down—which I often did—you came, on the right, to the sprawling campus of Renford Central School, and on the left, to a sprawling, rather upscale development, Renford Estates. It was in Renford Estates that most of my friends lived. But immediately to your left there was a clubhouse-pool-courts complex; "the courts"—as they were known—were a basketball court and a tennis court side by side. At age eight or nine I was judged old enough to walk down to the courts alone, and it was there, all the way through high school and even a little beyond it, that I spent much of my time, playing the game I loved.

My best friend in those years was Gene, a very bright guy who loved science and math and—unluckily—moved away in sixth grade. It was at his house in Renford Estates that—perhaps in fourth grade—he introduced me to chess. That became—but only for a few years, before I lost interest in it—another love of mine. Gene had a couple of books with notated games by the masters. I borrowed them, sat in my room over an old chess set we had, and played out the games in utter fascination. I quickly got good; Gene's analytical intelligence was formidable but I could give him competition, which he relished.

And along with basketball and chess, there was writing. One thing I did not like was school; if there was something I could tolerate, it was the story of the frontier conquests and wars of American history, of the tide pushing westward. I also loved to watch Westerns on TV. My enthusiasm for the romance of pioneering and armed conflicts was such that I started scrawling made-up pioneer stories and Westerns—lots of them—in notebooks. The pioneer stories featured Dave Harper, a kid living on the Kentucky frontier; the Westerns had adult, gunslinging protagonists. At any rate, while chess and even, eventually, basketball fell by the wayside, the writing habit— along with derivatives of it, like editing and translating—has stayed, and allowed me to eke some shekels out of the world.

My parents' bedroom was at one end of the one-story house; Nellie's and my bedrooms were at the other end, in what had been a garage till the previous owners converted it. Her room looked out on the driveway; mine had a view of the lilac hedge behind the house. Was it that distance from our parents' room, the feeling of being separate from them and on our own— but together—that made Nellie and me close? Or just some affinity? Whatever it was, we've been close as long as I can remember—and have managed to sustain it, if sporadically, during these decades I've been in Israel.

When we were children she would sometimes, when we were supposed to be going to sleep, come into my bed and we would lie there and talk. Why did she come into my bed instead of me going to hers? I think it was because—even though I was a year older—it was I who was afraid of the dark, something she sensed.

One night—we were probably aged around ten and nine—we heard the Randy Waite gang whiz past in their car, rock and roll blaring on the radio. We could be sure it was them; Renford Park was still small then, and they were the only juvenile-delinquent gang who did things like whiz around in a car at late hours, sometimes throwing beer cans on people's lawns.

I said, "Randy Waite."

"Yeah."

"What a bunch of crazy guys."

"Yeah."

"Why do they do things like that?"

"You said it."

"What'd I say?"

"Crazy. They're crazy. That's why they do things like that."

We both stared up in the dark.

I said, "When I get to be their age, I'm not going to do stuff like that."

"No?"

"Nope."

"What are you going to do?"

"I'm going to be…basketball star of the school."

"Yeah?"

"Yup."

"You're not that good now."

"I'm pretty good. I'm one of the best in intramurals."

"That's not what you said the other day. You said you were lousy in the semifinals."

"Well…I had a bad day. Anybody can have a bad day."

"So you're going to be great?"

"Yup."

"Steve Sandorsky, all-star of the world."

"That's right."
"All-star of the universe."
"Even better."
"Yeah, sure."
"Hey you, shut up."

We moved to Renford Park because my father got a job as lecturer, and later professor, in theoretical physics at RPI, a technical university in the nearby town of Troy. And there he worked for the remaining 20 years of his life. I wouldn't be able to tell you what he researched and wrote articles about; certainly I never talked with him about it while he was alive. Since his death I've made a few attempts to delve into it, but it's pretty much an incomprehensible bramble for the layman.

My father was a Jew who, late in 1938 when he was 15, was sent in a Kindertransport from Vienna to Britain. The Kindertransport was a program during the run-up and early part of World War II in which Jewish children and teenagers, mostly from Germany and Austria, were sent for refuge to Britain. The British weren't too careful about placing the kids with British families, and my father's experience with "his" family seems to have been negative. This was something we inferred from the fact that he almost never talked about it and had no contact with them; after he died, my mother told me he had told even her very little about it.

Although at first my father, an only child, corresponded from Britain with his parents in Vienna, the letters dwindled once the war started, then stopped altogether after a couple of years; it turned out his parents were shipped to a ghetto in

Lithuania where they died. After the war my father emigrated by himself to the U.S.

He was not only silent about his parents, and about his years in Britain, but tight-lipped in general, though in his last years there was one subject he would talk with me about—Israel. To this day I don't know how much his reserve was just part of his personality and how much it came from difficult realities, though it seems certain that trauma had something to do with it.

My mother—a curious, eager, practical, extroverted person—grew up in New York City and was of Presbyterian background. When she met my father he was a graduate student in physics at City College of New York; she was an undergrad, studying education. She told me—after he died—that they both kept coming to the same cafeteria at a time of day—midmorning—when they were almost the only ones there. She felt fascination and attraction toward him; it was she who got it going, sitting down with him one day at his table.

In one way they had it easy: the religion issue wasn't an issue for them. Trish Ainslee came from a mildly religious home; she was taken to church and the like. Basically it didn't interest her. She told me she thought we were here to live the lives we were given, and try to make the most of them; if there was something beyond that—which she doubted—she felt she didn't have time, or maybe even patience, for it.

In Arnold Sandorsky there was—I believe; about him I can mainly just conjecture—a much deeper alienation from religion. His parents appear to have been secular, assimilated Jews; the fact that they gave him a non-Jewish name like Arnold, and had non-Jewish first names themselves, would indicate that. Quite possibly, things that happened didn't dispose him to put stock in a benign Creator. In any case, his extent of Jewish "practice"—as far as I knew—was that he would not go to work on Rosh Hashanah and Yom Kippur. He did, though, toward the end, start to care rather intensely about Israel.

So this was the man my mother was married to—deep, seclusive, with grey eyes that seemed to ponder you solemnly. He worked long hours at RPI, and at home he had a study—a room with a desk and bookshelves, diagonal to their bedroom, at the end of the hall at the other side of the house—where he spent a good part of his time when he was home. And he smoked; smoked cigarettes constantly, a habit that apparently began while he was living with the family in Britain. "Different" and intriguing though he may have been to my mother, I don't think, in the end, what she really needed was a man who dwelt within himself so much, pursuing researches you couldn't connect with, harboring memories and scars that he surrounded with secrecy. And indeed—though she and my father did not fight and appeared basically to get along—she always seemed happier to me with Ed, her second husband up until she died in 2012.

Around when we moved to Renford, my mother started taking night courses at a nearby college to upgrade her BA in education to an MA. And as soon as Nellie started going to kindergarten, she got a job as guidance counselor in one of the area's high schools. At the supper table she would regale us with stories about the people there—kids she counseled, friends, bosses—even though, I'm afraid, none of us had a great interest in what she was saying. My mother liked to talk; but perhaps the chatter was also a way of skirting, of deflecting and coping with, the silence of Arnold Sandorsky.

One rarely went into my father's study while he was there, apart from brief "Dad, Mom says supper's ready" missions and the like. But sometimes I went into it when he wasn't there.

The first time was a day during—third grade?—when I stayed home from school with a cold or low fever or something like that, and was judged old enough to manage without my mother being there.

A quiet autumn morning with a grey sky, dusky light seeping through the windows. I think it was about midmorning when the idea of going there seemed to infiltrate and conquer me, and I found myself walking there through the dark hall.

Their picture—Louis and Greta Sandorsky—was perched on the ledge of a bookshelf. I saw that, from where he sat at the desk, he faced it directly and could see it by slightly lifting his gaze. Did it just become part of the ambience as pictures will? Did he look at it a lot?

I could see it by standing at eye-level with it. These were my grandparents. They seemed old enough that it was close to the time—late 1938—when Arnold left them for Britain. In sepia tones, Louis is wearing a jacket and tie, Greta a flowery dress. If I can see a similarity to my father in either of them, it's in Louis's high forehead and curly hair, though his hair seems grey. Both of them look at the camera with a pleasant, accommodating expression. If they had an awareness of political deterioration and danger, it doesn't show in the picture; they seem serenely content. Greta has short, dark hair parted in the middle. Louis's eyes are lighter, gently astute; Greta's are dark, rich with modulated emotion.

I remember another of the nighttime talks with Nellie, lying beside each other, staring upward, not looking at each other. I'm not sure when this one was; it could well have been when I was in fifth grade, the time when I went most often into my father's study alone, and was the most occupied with the subject.

"Hey, did you ever go in Dad's study when Dad's not there?"

"Hah? Why would I go in there when he's not there?"

"Well, you can see the picture."

"The picture of Dad's parents?"

"Yup."

"So. I can see it when he's there."

"Yeah but…when he's not there…like, you can really look at it."

"Yeah?"

"Yeah."

"So that's what you do, you snoop around?"

"Yup. Sometimes."

"So, what do you see when you see the picture when he's not there that you can't see when he's there?"

"Well. You can get to know them better."

"Get to *know* them better."

"Yup."

"But they're dead."

"Well. You can see what they were like."

"Yeah?"

"Yeah."

"So what were they like?"

"Well, they were calm."

"They were calm?"

"Yup."

"Well, so what?"

"Well, it was a weird time to be calm. Because things were getting kind of bad."

"So maybe they didn't know."

"Well, I kind of think they did."

"Yeah?"

"Yeah."

"Well, I don't think I wanna do that. I don't think I wanna go in and look at them like that."

"No?"

"Nope."

"Why not?"

"I don't know, it's kind of sad. I think I'd feel sad to look at them."

"So what's the big deal about that?"

"I don't know. I don't like to feel sad."

Of course, I had living grandparents too—Clyde and Dorothy Ainslee. Retired, they had an apartment in Manhattan; sometimes we went down there to visit them, but more often they came up to visit us. My parents were very busy, while Grandpa and Grandma had time on their hands; also I think they got a kick out of seeing us—Nellie and me in particular—in what could be called our natural setting, a place so surprisingly rural after so many years in the city.

There was an advantage to getting together with them: one got to see my father talking. Clyde Ainslee was big, florid, with wispy white hair; and he was a talker. He had worked as a machinist, and apparently had been active in the union. Although I never took part in these conversations, Grandpa had a loud, declarative voice, and there was the anomaly of Dad talking as well, so I couldn't help sometimes tuning in. Grandpa's main focus was New York City politics, and especially his bitterness over what he saw as the ongoing injustices suffered by the machinists' and other unions. Dad preferred a larger canvas—Kennedy, Johnson, Castro, Khrushchev. But they could work out enough common ground to chat successfully for quite long times. And they were both Democrats, though later Dad turned more conservative.

Meanwhile Mom and Grandma sat "with them"—it was usually in the backyard—but not really with them, consolidating into their own garrulous island, facing each other in their chairs. About these hushed, rapid parleys I can report nothing; I could hardly hear what they were saying, and even when I could, I bounced off it indifferently. Dorothy Ainslee was a small woman with high cheekbones and a startled look; she had worked, I believe, as a nurse.

And, of course, they both took a great interest in their grandchildren (they also had two others, but my mother's sister lived in Seattle and they didn't see them much). Grandpa, who assumed that men are basically concerned with the public sphere, would ask me implacably about school—the sphere of life that least interested me. Asked what my favorite subject was and the like, I would mutter something like "social studies," even though actually I found almost all of school an insufferable imposition. Sports may have offered more common ground, but when he found out that I was a Boston Celtics rather than New York Knicks fan, it truly disturbed him and after that he would approach the subject only gingerly. Toward Nellie his attitude was more intense, actually fierce: "Little *girl…*!" he'd say and always grab her, put her on his knee, and beam at her there, Nellie's face conveying a mix of flattery and embarrassment.

Grandma, too, melted at the sight of Nellie; she would ask her questions and melt at the answers, Nellie's face conveying awareness that the content of her words did not matter.

Toward me, too, Grandma's eyes exuded keen enthusiasm, but her attempts to converse with me were generally even more awkward than Grandpa's.

After Dad died, my mother told me that at first her parents weren't happy about him as a prospective son-in-law. They weren't anti-Jewish, Mom said, but—despite their own lukewarm involvement—they wanted her to stay within Presbyterianism, or at least Protestantism, or at least Christianity. They also didn't have much confidence in Dad as a provider; in those days, with his unkempt look, he gave the impression of a dreamy, impractical egghead. On that count they gradually got reassured, of course, as it turned out he was a successful academic and responsible—though remote—person.

But if the yard with the pool, the sight of the cornfield, could weave an idyllic spell, the true essence of the idyllic was to be found at Pohawnsee Lake. Small, a bit north of Lake George in the Adirondack Mountains, each year my parents rented a summer cottage there for about two weeks, and one day each summer we'd pile into the car with all the packed bags, leave suburbia and farmland behind, and drive less than two hours north into, so to speak, the wilderness. We'd take our cat Tom with us for a sojourn in paradise, hunting birds in pine woods. We were there for the last time when I was thirteen; then the owners sold the place and we saw it no more.

Pohawnsee Lake was blue and bright and surrounded by pine-covered mountains. There was a small beach with a dock, a rowboat, and a raft rocking in the ripples. The mountain air was sweet and pure, heavy with the pine scent at early morning or dusk. Nellie and I could play in the water—swimming, climbing up on the raft and riding it as it rocked, jumping from it—endlessly; the joy was simply infinite. The cottage was one of a group of five or six, and sometimes there were other kids we played with. At night you saw the sky in a way you hadn't seen it elsewhere, the stars incredibly multitudinous and brilliant.

But this was also the place where, in my whole childhood, I came closest to getting to know—to having some substantial contact with—my father. There were two things we did together there that interested us, specifically, and not so much Nellie or Mom: rowboat rides and playing chess.

My father liked rowboat rides—a chance to drift serenely, to contemplate. I liked them—I think it's simply because I love water, bodies of water, being near them, being on them. "Steve, want to take the rowboat out?" For the other boys I knew, boys whose fathers routinely took them to toss a football back and forth or shoot baskets together at a driveway hoop, such words may have been pleasant but ordinary. For me they were a thrilling summons.

We didn't talk much in these outings; even to me there didn't seem much need for it. My father rowed, looking out at the lake, the mountains, with an expression as if he was surveying the scene and was favorably impressed with it. The bluish smoke drifting up seemed part of the placidity. Sometimes he let me row, which meant executing the complicated task of changing places in a rowboat. His face—rectangular and broad, with the high forehead, grey eyes, and stolid mouth—looked less forbidding, seemed to disclose a tacit gentleness. When people passed in a motorboat, often with a trailing water skier, they always waved; my father smiled and waved back.

Once he said, "This place is very old."

I said, "What, the lake?"

He said, "The lake is *very* old. But there was a settlement here already in Revolutionary War days."

I sought for something to say, but didn't find anything; even though I had a lot of feelings about what he'd said—how it must have been back then, the leafy pristine quietude.

And as for chess, I think he played it with me there because he lacked his study and needed something else a bit challenging to fill the time. Our main activity in the evening was Scrabble for all four of us; a game I also liked. But sometimes after the Scrabble game, or in a lethargic span of time during the day, he'd say, "Steve, feel like playing some chess?"—or just, with a suggestive glance at me, set the board and box of pieces on the cottage's dining room table if I was sitting there or near there.

You could beat Gene sometimes, but you could not beat Dad. When I say he sought something a little challenging, I mean that I was sometimes—at best—able to put up some competition and make him think in order to win. This was, of course, despite the fact that for many years he had never played chess except for two weeks each year at Pohawnsee Lake. How far back did he and chess go?—New York? Britain? Vienna? I have never known and never will; of course, he didn't disclose to me his personal history with chess.

And yet those hours spent playing with him were revelatory in a way; revelatory of things—good things—about him that I rarely saw otherwise. The way his bearing, his expression, his few words, quietly conveyed a respect for me as a player, for the moves I made—and, simply, for me; a courtly, very decent sort of respect that made you feel valued and good. The way he seemed surprised, even a touch apologetic, when he took advantage of an unwise move on my part, or executed a devastating move that he'd long been planning but that my radar hadn't prophesied; an attitude that seemed to express real awareness of, real consideration for the other person, and real humility on his part.

And, of course, he smoked; sometimes he'd preface a move with a last puff, a look of shrewd calculation.

2

"Amy," Nellie said one night, "says Chanukah is better than Christmas."

"Yeah? Why does she say that?"

It was a night when I was in sixth grade, Nellie in fifth. It was December, snow outside, the air pleasantly cold as we lay under the quilt. Amy Goldberg was in Nellie's grade and was her best friend. Though the school was large, encompassing the town, the developments, and miles of rural homes and farms, Amy was one of only a tiny number of Jewish kids in it.

"It's eight days long. And you get presents every day."

"Presents every day?"

"Yup."

"I don't believe that."

"Well, that's what she says."

I said, "So why don't we have Chanukah?"

She made a small sound of amazement.

"You don't know that?"

"No."

"Because we're *not Jews*."

I said, "Not Jews?"

"Nope."

"What do you mean?"

"Amy says you're only Jewish if your mother's Jewish. That's the Jewish rule."

"But Dad's Jewish."

"I know. But…he's Dad. You're only Jewish if your mom's Jewish."

"I don't believe that."

She laughed.

"So what."

"What do you mean, so what?"

"It doesn't matter what you believe."

"Yeah it does."

"No it doesn't."

"Yeah it does."

"No it doesn't."

"How can you not be Jewish if your dad's Jewish?"

"I don't know. But that's the rule."

"Why, because Amy says it is?"

"Yeah, don't you think she might know?"

"Well what if I don't like this rule?"

"So, don't like it. No, you know what? You can change all the rules. You can make everything just the way you want it. You can be the Wizard of Oz."

That conversation would have been in December 1965. I was toward the end of childhood; things were changing. Kids in my class were "going steady"; I observed this phenomenon—an unrelated boy and girl being together a lot, wanting to be together a lot, even hugging and kissing—with fascination, with wonderment. The TV comedy *Gilligan's Island* was then in its heyday; the character Mary Ann gave me feelings that

I didn't—yet—associate with the boys and girls hugging and kissing, not yet seeing the connection. It was in this period that Nellie started coming less and less to my bed at night, until—by about the end of that school year—she stopped altogether. It was something we both tacitly understood had to cease, while remaining close friends.

The conversation with her that winter night put me in a dark mood. One result was that I stopped—as I'd been doing for a few years—stealing into my father's study, when I was alone in the house, to look at the picture of my grandparents. They always seemed to welcome me. They seemed gently pleased that someone was coming to visit them in their extended quietude. Louis's look seemed appreciative; Greta's seemed richly contemplative, as if mulling the fact that this grandson was so attentive.

Many years later, while I was living in Jerusalem, I searched for my grandparents at the website of Yad Vashem, the Holocaust museum in Jerusalem. I found out that: they were deported from Vienna, the train headed for the Kovno ghetto in Lithuania, on November 23, 1941. The datum for Louis said that he "died there on November 29, 1941." I further found out that on that day, November 29, 1941, five thousand Jews who had been shipped to Kovno from Berlin, Munich, Frankfurt, Vienna, and Breslau—two thousand of them from Vienna—were killed in a mass shooting at the Ninth Fort, very soon after stepping off the trains. It appears just about certain that Louis was one of them. The fact that the same datum doesn't appear beside Greta's name probably just means that, while she met the same fate, it wasn't recorded. Or, if she kept living for a while and had a different fate, there appears to be no record of what it was.

The picture—more than anything that happened during a couple of weeks each year at Pohawnsee Lake—was my closest communion with my father. Whether he looked at it often or not didn't matter; it was the fact that he must have done so at least sometimes. He looked at it; I did; all of us—the three generations—were in a communion, a Jewish communion. What Nellie told me that night—in utter, blithe ignorance of its impact on me—stunned me with the feeling that I wasn't really part of it, had never been. It was something that had happened to Jews; but I was not—she said, Amy said—a Jew.

I was in a dark mood even though there was bright snow on the ground and Christmas was approaching. Christmas: in the morning Nellie and I would eagerly dig our presents out from under the tree, tear the wrapping off the boxes. The image: Mom is kneeling beside us, watching with enthusiasm, commenting; Dad is standing in the background, his arms folded, looking on with something like a dim smile. From far in the future, I'd say that—until that year—I felt that I was a Jew doing something not-Jewish, doing it because I liked it and because Mom was a Christian. We didn't go to church—or synagogue—ever. Churches and synagogues were something that Nellie and I heard about, or sometimes saw on a TV or movie screen, but had never seen from the inside.

That year, though, when Christmas came, I opened my presents more listlessly—even though getting presents still had the power to thrill me.

After a few days of my morose frame of mind, still before Christmas, I came home from school one day, went to the kitchen and extracted a piece of cake from the breadbox and a glass of orange juice from the refrigerator, went around the partition and sat at the table. My mother happened to be there, drinking coffee and scanning the local paper with her glasses on. The windows there looked out at the lilac hedge, now a brown bramble couched in snow. Just outside one window there was a birdhouse, mounted on the wall, where chickadees now fluttered.

I elaborately sat down, arranged my cake and juice before me, and went to work—diffidently—on them.

"Well," Mom said, without looking up from her page. It was a very general statement, meaning, "I see you're here. Anything interesting happen today? Tell me about it." Mom had straight, dark blond hair cascading neatly from her oval head to her shoulders. She had high cheekbones like her mother, bright, active blue eyes, a small, tight, resolute mouth.

A couple more minutes may have passed before I said, "Was talking with Nellie the other day."

She stopped; of course catching that my tone wasn't usual.

"She said something weird."

Still holding the paper—but in a kind of suspension—she ventured a dim, tentative smile.

"Weird?"

"Yeah, I don't know."

I concentrated on cutting off a piece of cake with my fork, lifting it to my mouth—as if reluctantly—and chewing it.

"I don't know. She said...you're only Jewish if your mother's Jewish, not just if your father is."

Mom's face showed a certain perplexity now as she lowered the newspaper to the table, settled her chin in her hand, and looked at me intently.

"Well," she finally said, "as I understand it, that's true."

I said—still diligently eating my cake—"Seems like a weird rule."

She smiled. "Well, when a lady has a baby, everyone knows for sure that she's the mom."

36

She said, "Jews have lots of rules, I guess. You know, ko-sher, that kind of thing."

I loudly pushed back my chair; took my dishes back around the partition to the sink.

"Steve?" I heard her say.

"Yeah."

"You seem a little…disturbed about this."

"No, it's all right. I was just curious."

I walked back to where she was, went past her without looking at her; down the steps to the breezeway and into my room.

From the brightness—in general—of childhood I stepped into an adolescent world that was darker. I was sick of school, but secretly perturbed to see my grades decline as I did less and less homework, paid less and less attention in class; crazed by the sight of girls, but unable to get real satisfaction for the feelings; bitter about not being a Jew, but not believing that I could belong to anything else, that I could be in anything but a no man's land. In retrospect, it would have been better if Gene hadn't moved away; without him (until the summer when I was sixteen), though I was chummy with lots of guys, I didn't have a real, close friend in school, someone I could really talk to.

The brainier kids in my class were generally the grade-grub-bing kind—I think the word *nerd* was just then coming into use—and as my marks went downhill I drifted away from them, not finding them too appealing in any case. Instead, as I turned into a pretty good basketball player at ages thir-teen-fourteen, I naturally melded into the world of athletic guys who hung around the courts, sometimes just shooting baskets and engaging in gruff talk, sometimes choosing sides and having serious games. That was best—immersing myself in the games, having clear goals: winning the game, sinking long jump shots, which I was good at. Going with this crowd meant encountering lots of beer—at the courts themselves, at parties, or just roaming around in the streets; by that time a lot of the kids in Renford Park, not just a gang or two, were quite wild. And like innumerable morose, frustrated people, I took to beer, and stronger drinks—excessively. It was a habit that stayed with me, worse, of course, when I was feeling down, or under pressure; though in recent years I've totally kicked it, apart from maybe a glass of wine when we go out.

July 21-22, 1970

3

In a summer evening, I was shooting baskets alone at the courts. I knew that other guys—someone or other—would show up and we'd have a game.

The courts were pleasant at the dusk hour. The nets of the two basketball hoops—one at either end of the basketball court—looked delicately white against the backdrop of greyish blue. The sound of the ball on the pavement had a special resonance. The cool air made me feel infinitely springy, made me whirl and jump as if in the deciding game of the NBA playoffs.

It was the summer after tenth grade; I'd turned sixteen in the spring. Before that I'd been on the JV basketball team—not a starter, but a guard who came off the bench for not-negligible playing time. I wasn't at all sure I'd make the varsity team in the fall; or if I did make it, it seemed certain that I'd be no more than a benchwarmer. It was part of what I saw as a pattern of failure and pointlessness.

A car pulled up in the gravel at one end of the court—the end closer to the pool and the clubhouse, looking into the development. I tucked my ball under my arm and strode over to see who it was. The car doors slammed—sharp cracks in the dusk—and four people came out. Jimmy Boynton, the driver. Stu Westervelt. Doug Peck. Connie Landry.

As they came around the wire-mesh fence and onto the court, Jimmy said, "Sandorsky, you son-of-a-bitching Polack, what the fuck are you doing here?"

Even though one of them, Doug, had a basketball, Jimmy came over and batted mine away, dribbled it to the basket and made a flamboyant lay-up. Jimmy—now seventeen and old enough to drive at night—had been on the varsity team during the year, but had been permanently kicked off all teams after a coach had caught him drinking whiskey in the locker room. He had a muscular, bowlegged build, a face like a terrier, thick brown hair that bounced as he walked.

"OK," he said, "me and Sandorsky against you guys."

"Yeah, fuck that," said Doug. "You guys'll fuckin' mutilate us."

Doug was tall and could sort of play basketball, though he'd never been on a team. Stu was a stocky footballer, not built for basketball.

"OK, Peck, you get Sandorsky," said Jimmy. "Come on, Westervelt, I'm going to teach you how to fuckin' play this game."

"Hi, Steve!"

It was Connie; she'd sat down in the grass beside the court, hugging her knees.

I said, "Hey Connie, how you doin'."

It was fun and exhilarating to play against Jimmy. I couldn't outplay him but I made him work hard; he honored me with many epithets. Because the gap in ability between Doug and Stu was greater than the gap between Jimmy and me, for a while it seemed we might win. Then, with the score 9-9, Jimmy made a driving lay-up; then stole the ball from Doug and instantly converted it into a winning jump shot.

"Oh, you fuck," said Doug.

As we'd been playing, the court's floodlights had come on. Jeff LaBelle and some guys had materialized there at the left corner of the court, after rounding the fence. They were all good basketball players, though some of them—like Jimmy—had been barred from being on teams. One of them, Marty Frear, was a buddy of mine; he said, "Hey, Steve!" and I said, "Hey, Marty!"

Now as they walked onto the court, holding beer cans, Jeff said, "Boynton, you stupid fuck. I'm gonna whip your ass."

"Sandorsky," Jimmy said, "let's you and me whip these fuckers' asses."

"Nah," I said. "I'm gonna take a break."

"Take a break, what the fuck you gonna do that for."

"He wants to talk to Landry," Doug said under his breath.

Stu said something else under his breath.

I was already walking toward her. She was still sitting there hugging her knees, looking small and demure.

I stood over her and said, "Hey Connie, what's doin'."

She squinted up at me, the light from the floodlight on her face, and said, "Steve."

I sat down beside her. On the court they'd chosen up sides, a three-on-three with Stu excluded, watching from behind the basket. Jimmy started the game, dribbling the ball hard on the pavement in a crouch.

Connie was in my grade. I didn't know her, but I knew that, whenever we were near each other, she looked at me. I knew that tonight, while we were playing ball, she'd been doing it too. I also knew that she was an only child, which in those days was still quite rare. She was of petite build, with auburn, bushy hair down to the middle of her back, a small, feminine face with green eyes under very graceful—strikingly so—eyebrows. That night she wore a green sleeveless top and loose, fringed denim shorts. Despite being good-looking she wasn't part of the large swath of good-looking girls who either were or wanted to be cheerleaders, but she wasn't so much with the nerdy, brainy kids either; she was considered an uncertain quantity, somewhat apart, deep, different.

"Connie," I said. "What were you doing riding in a car with jerks like these."

She peered sideways at me. "You don't like your friends?"

"Who says they're my friends?"

"Then why do you hang out with them?"

"You got someone else I can play basketball with?"

"Steve, why are you so cynical?"

"I don't know, God must have made me this way."

She said, "Jimmy said, 'Hey Connie, want a ride?' I said, 'Where you going?' He said, 'Why don't you come in and find out?' So. I found out."

"Didn't they bother you?"

"Come on. Stu said stupid things. You can swat him like a fly."

"So were you thrilled when you found out where they were going?"

"Oh yeah, Steve. Big thrill."

She said, "But then I said…well, look who's here. If it isn't Steve."

"Well," I said. "Guess it isn't all bad."

On the court there was a lot of noise of ball on pavement, ball rattling the rim, curses. The sky was now deep blue with first pale stars strewn in it.

"Steve."

"Yeah."

"Anyone ever tell you you need a haircut?"

"Yeah. My mom tells me."

She reached out, for a moment, and toyed with hair at the side of my head.

"It's all right. I like it."

"Yeah?"

"Yeah. It's cute."

I touched my hair as if to confirm it. "Well, that's good."

We both looked at the court where there was now a semiserious altercation between Jimmy and Jeff, Jimmy claiming Jeff had fouled him, Jeff denying it.

She said, "You never talk to me in school."

I looked contemplatively at her. "Well, I don't know you."

"So. How do you get to know people?"

"I don't know, Connie, it's a big school. It's got hundreds of people in it. I don't get to talk to everyone."

She smiled wanly into a distance. "*Such* a typical thing for a guy to say. It's all numbers, right? The odds are just…too high, so you couldn't talk to me."

"Yeah, what can I say Connie. Maybe I've been hanging around these guys too much, and it's made me kind of a moron."

I said, "But we're talking now, aren't we?"

"Yeah. At last."

They'd gotten squared away on the court and were playing grimly again.

She said, "My mother is a jerk."

"Your mother?"

"I'm in my room listening to my Janis Ian album. It wasn't loud at all. You'd believe me if you were there. She comes banging on my door… '*Turn that down! Don't you know I have a headache?*'"

45

"Ha-ha."

"So. I make a big mistake. I go to the door, I open it, I say, 'Mom, it's *not loud.*' You don't want to do that with my mom. You don't want to challenge anything that she says. Never question anything that the Queen on High has spoken. Not when she's like that."

"Yeah, what'd she do?"

"Aa…" She waved her hand derisively.

She said, "'*I work, I work for you all day, I work to support you, and I come home with a splitting headache from a day of work and all I want to do is rest, and you blare your stereo so I can't even do that, and I dare, I dare, to politely request that you turn it down, and you have the nerve to get fresh with me and argue with me.*'"

I said, "Sounds like a peach."

"And all this is, you know, at two hundred decibels, and she's got this high whiny voice that just cuts right through you. So I said, I don't need this, and I just got out of there. I just walked right out of there and walked around in the street. I didn't give a damn about anything anymore. Then these guys come along and offer me a ride. I couldn't have cared less where they were going. I would have been happy if they drove off a cliff. And then they come here, and…you're here."

She sat very still.

I reached out and held her forearm.

"Steve."

"Yeah?"

She said nothing else.

I let go of her arm—not wanting the guys to see it and talk about it.

I said, "We should get out of here."

On the court the game was winding up, still with recriminations between Jimmy and Jeff. Jimmy came walking over to us. He stood with his arms folded looking down at us, a bit like an army commander checking soldiers at a post.

He said, "Sandorsky, you got a couple of bills?"

I said, "What the hell do you want my money for, Boynton?"

"I'm gonna drive down to QuickMart. Get us some beer there. I'll get you a six-pack."

"They won't sell it to you."

"Yeah, they will. Randy Waite got a job there. He'll sell beer to all of us."

I looked at Connie. Jimmy's offer was tempting; I was thirsty, and the beer would have tasted wonderful.

I said, "No thanks, Jimmy."

"Why the fuck not?"

"I don't know. Next time."

"Fuck it. Your problem."

He looked at us once more. He started to walk away; he tossed over his shoulder, "Looks like you got other things to do."

I said, "What do you say, Connie? Get out of this place?"

She took my hand in hers, entwined the fingers.

"Steve, where do you want to take me."

"Atlantic City."

"Atlantic *City*! Let's go."

"I don't know, Con, let's just walk around and see where we end up."

The moon had risen, shedding a cottony light on the field where summer-camp kids engaged in archery and badminton during the day, and where we now walked far from the courts, far enough that, even if they'd resumed playing, we couldn't have heard them. I'd left my basketball with Marty. The clubhouse-pool buildings, which we could now see from a distance, could have been structures of an ancient city under the spectral light.

I came to a point where I stopped walking. We were arm in arm, and she, of course, stopped too. What happened next wasn't initiated by me, or her; it was synchronous. It went on, and on, and on; I would have stopped, but she couldn't.

Finally I said, "Connie."

She was still breathing deep, her eyes closed.

I said, "It's nice here."

It's very awkward to try to convey to someone, without saying it outright, that you want the two of you to lie down; I tugged at her arm, while sinking slightly myself.

"Steve."

"Yeah?"

"I don't like it here."

"You don't like it?"

"It's too open."

She had a point; kids who were drinking beer and the like walked around here at night.

I said, "So where do you want to go?"

"Well. We could go to my house."

"Your house? What about…"

"My mom?"

"Yeah."

"My mom is a problem…. She gets drunk at night."

"She gets drunk?"

"Yeah… Damn. I could show you my cat. I could play you my records…. Damn. If only she wasn't there."

I said, "What about the golf course?"

She was giving me a look. I couldn't make it out in the dimness.

I said, "It's quiet there."

She said, "You should know, Steve."

"I should know?"

"Yeah."

"What do you mean by that?"

"Well. You and Becky Furlow should know."

"You *heard* about that?"

"Yeah."

"How did you hear about that?"

"Girls talk about things like that."

"Oh. Guys do too…I guess in a different way."

"Steve."

She was staring at me pretty seriously.

"I'm not looking for that."

"It's all right, Connie. I'm not either. You don't have to worry. I just…want to go there. It's nice there."

"Steve."

"All right, look, if that's what you wanted to do, I wouldn't stage a protest demonstration against it. But…it's all right. It's not the teacher's assignment."

She gave an abrupt laugh.

"You have a weird way of putting things."

"Yeah?"

"Yeah. But it's all right."

Under the stars, under the summer night, Renford Estates was quiet. We passed the hulking forms of houses, one by one. The moon had climbed over the highest tree-level and taken over, solitary, supreme, spreading its light. I could see—by peering intently at my watch—that it was past nine. I was supposed to be home by eleven. I knew that—even if we didn't stay long at the golf course, which didn't seem likely—in the time it would take to walk there, be there, walk Connie home, and walk home myself, the clock would progress well past eleven. It wasn't good, but I knew I wasn't going to do anything about it.

I said, "So what does your mom do?"

I was walking with my arm around her, her head resting on my shoulder; she seemed to have to bestir herself, lifting her head.

"My mom?"

She said, "My mom. Let's see. When she's not getting drunk and having fits? She works as a dentist's assistant."

"A dentist's assistant. I hope she doesn't get drunk while she's doing that."

"I hope so too. But I wouldn't put anything past her."

"Where's your dad?"

She gave a sharp, high laugh.

"My dad. Let's see. I think he's out bowling with the boys. No, I think he's at a PTA meeting."

She said, "My dad lives in Cleveland. He's been living there since I was in fifth grade."

"What, they're divorced?"

"They are now. But they weren't then. He just flew the coop one day."

"Yeah?"

I thought to say something like, "Considering your mother, I guess it's understandable," but thought better of it.

I said, "So, you in touch?"

"In touch. In touch."

She said, "My father's a worse jerk than my mother. He calls me maybe once a year."

"Oh."

I said, "I'm sorry to hear that."

"But there was something good about it when he took off."

"Something good?"

"Until then I had to go to a Catholic school. After that, I didn't have to anymore."

"Wait. He made you go to a Catholic school, and then he just...took off like that?"

"My father...is a beacon of moral righteousness."

"Sounds that way."

The golf course bordered a long, pretty wide pond, and we'd reached the part of the road where the houses gave out and there was just a steel fence on either side; beyond the fence, on either side, the murky darkness where there were marsh grasses and pools of water.

She said, "So why aren't you with Becky?"

"With *Becky?*"

I said, "That was a couple of months ago."

"A couple of months. Wow."

"Connie...it wasn't some love story or something."

I said, "We were at a party at Deb Fisher's, right around here. We were both drunk. We went out for a walk together."

I said, "She wanted to get back at Rick. Rick's got some girl in Belmont he fools around with."

"So, that's it? Helping her get back at Rick?"

"No. Connie, I don't know what you want me to say."

She stopped walking, got loose from me, turned and faced me.

She was looking at me with an expression that—I could just make out—had something distant and speculative about it.

"So you just do that without it meaning anything to you?"

"No."

I said, "There was never anything deep between me and Becky. We were drunk. It was just something that happened."

"You should have let Jimmy buy you that beer."

"I didn't want to. I didn't want to be drinking beer tonight, Connie."

I put my hands on her shoulders. She stood there neutrally; I managed to put an end to the line of questioning.

In the soft, fragrant grass by the willows beside the pond, we were, for a while, quiet—more or less, though I stayed within the limit she'd set, didn't try to test it.

After that we lay on our backs, my right hand holding her left hand. The moon was high, the stars bright. The pond beside us was in a deep calm; there was just an intermittent, slow, pensive sound from a frog like a bass string being plucked.

She said, "I wish there was just this."

"Just this?"

"Yeah. I wish there wasn't a world out there, and there was nothing but this."

"It's really quiet...maybe it went away."

"What, the world?"

"Yeah."

"Doubt it."

"We can check later. See if it's still there."

She said, "You know the story in the Bible where God tells Noah he's fed up?"

"I've heard about it."

"'I will destroy man from the earth. I'm really sorry I made him. The earth is full of violence. I'm going to get rid of all of them.'"

"But he lets Noah and his family get away in the ark, right?"

"Yeah, Noah and his family plus a male and a female of all the species."

"And when the rain stops, they all get it started all over again, right?"

"Right."

"So it doesn't do any good."

"Nope."

She said, "Do you know what time it is?"

Twisting and peering, I said, "It's something like eleven-fifteen."

She answered by sighing.

I said, "Your mother waiting for you?"

"There's no way of knowing. Most likely she's in her stupor. But, who knows."

She said, "What about you?"

"Oh, me. I'm sworn on ten Bibles to be back at eleven."

"Oh," she said.

She said, "Too bad."

"Yeah..."

"So, I assume there are a Mr. and Mrs. Sandorsky?"

"Yes, there are a Mr. and Mrs. Sandorsky."

"And what does Mr. Sandorsky do?"

"Mr. Sandorsky—Professor Sandorsky—is a professor of physics at RPI."

"A professor of physics at RPI?"

"Yup."

"Wow."

She said, "What kind of name is Sandorsky?"

"It's, uh...I don't know. Polish, Russian, something like that. It's Jewish."

She lay still.

"It's Jewish?"

"Yup."

She got up on one elbow and looked at me.

"You're Jewish?"

"You got a problem with it?"

"No, I don't have a problem with it. But...I'm amazed. All these years I didn't know that you're Jewish."

"Well, I'm not."

She looked at me.

"You just said your name's Jewish."

"It's my father's name. He's Jewish. I'm not."

"Wait. How can *you* not be if he is?"

"It's the Jewish rule. You're a Jew only if your mother's a Jew. Fathers don't count."

She kept staring at me; then got onto her back again.

She slid her left hand back into my right hand, put her right hand behind her head, pondering.

"It's because you can't tell for sure who the father is?"

"Something like that."

"So, your father...does he go to some temple?"

"No. He's totally nonreligious."

"What's he like?"

"Well, he's real quiet. I don't know that much about him."

"No?"

"No, he doesn't talk much."

"Doesn't talk much."

"Nope."

"And Mrs. Sandorsky is not a Jew."

"Nope."

"Is she a Catholic?"

"No. Presbyterian."

"So you're a Presbyterian."

"No. My mother's as totally nonreligious as my father is. I'm kind of a nothing."

"A nothing."

"Yeah."

She said, "So you're like in that poem, 'I'm nobody, who are you,' something like that?"

"Something like that."

"So that's who I'm with? Mr. Nothing and Nobody?"

"Yes, I'd say that's exactly who you're with."

"And what does Mrs. Sandorsky do, Mr. Nobody?"

"She's the guidance counselor at Guilderford, Miss Landry."

"Yeah?"

"Yeah."

"Well, this is impressive. Professor Sandorsky is a professor, and Mrs. Sandorsky guides all the kids at Guilderford."

"Right."

"Your sister's a real brain, too."

"Nellie? Yeah, she is."

"Wasn't she in tenth-grade classes this year?"

"In French, and in English. She's a whiz with languages. They started her in ninth-grade French, and it was like…she knew French, without having to learn it. I don't know how she does it. So they put her in tenth-grade French. And she was the star of that class."

"Wow."

We lay quiet for a while. She squeezed my hand; our fingers toyed with each other. The frog made the strange twanging sound.

"And what are you good at, Mr. Sandorsky, Jr., or Mr. Nobody, or whatever your name is."

"Me? I guess nothing, really. I'm not even that good at basketball."

"You seemed pretty good tonight."

"Aa. I won't even make varsity. I didn't even start on JV."

"Well, there are some things you're good at."

She ran her finger along the side of my hand.

"Well, that's good to know."

I said, "I used to be pretty good at chess when I was a kid. Then I lost interest in it. I guess basketball took over."

"Yeah?"

"Also I used to do a lot of writing. A hell of a lot of writing, when I was kid. I used to just fill up these notebooks with stories that I'd write, Westerns and things. Stopped that too."

She got up on her elbow again, looked at me.

"You stopped?"

"Yeah."

"They say that writing is something natural, something a person's born with."

"Well, it might be true. Maybe I'll start again someday."

"I do quite a lot of writing."

"You do?"

"Yeah, just this diary. I write in it every day. I really don't know why. Everything that happens to me, I write it down. Maybe so I can have enough evidence for the proceedings against my mother."

I looked at her with a smile, not knowing if she could see it.

I caressed her hair, her lips.

She said, "I always wanted you to talk to me."

"Yeah?"

"Yeah."

She said, "When I came to Renford from the Catholic school, in fifth grade...do you remember Mr. Barker's music class?"

"Oh, yeah. In that big room where the band practiced. They combined some classes for it."

"Right. I was sitting a few rows behind you, on those chairs, and I was always looking at you. Wondering what it would be like to talk to you. But…you don't remember, I'm sure."

"Connie, in all honesty… If you were sitting behind me, I don't have eyes in the back of my head."

"Oh, there we go. The boy logic again."

"Typical, right?"

"Right."

"According to the girl logic, I should have just known that you were looking at me, even though I couldn't see you."

"Right. Exactly."

She said, "What about all the other times?"

"What, that you were looking at me?"

"Yeah."

"Yes, Connie, I was aware of it. Why didn't you talk to me?"

"Well, you seemed in your own world. I didn't think you wanted me intruding on it in particular."

"So, you see, that's what I was like. In my own world. I really never had anything with girls until this last year or so."

"And in this last year you made up for it."

"Oh, not that much."

She lay back down again.

We lay there in the deep calm that had stilled the trees, the pond, looking at the stars.

She said, "Wish it could just be this."

"You almost sound depressed."

"Yeah, I have a talent at that."

She said, "If I really, really, have to go back to that world… that I've been assigned to live in…then there's one thing I'd really love to do in it."

"What's that?"

"I'd love to swim in your pool."

"My pool?"

"Yeah."

She said, "I love swimming, but…I never go to the Renford pool. Too noisy. Too crowded. But that pool you've got in your backyard…it's nice."

"Yeah, of course. It's not that big but…you can sort of swim in it."

I said, "Yeah, that would be great."

"What if I came tomorrow? Would that be OK?"

"Tomorrow? Sure."

"If they don't mind."

"No, why should they mind?"

"Maybe I can glimpse your mysterious father."

"You might."

"And say hi to your sister."

"There's a good chance of that."

"Such a nice person, on top of being smart."

"Yeah, she's all right."

"I must have done something really good. Things that I just hoped and dreamed about…seem to be happening."

"Yeah? So what did you do that was really good?"

"Well. Let me think. Not that much, I don't think. Oh, there was something. I adopted a stray cat."

"Yeah?"

"It was just this pathetic, beige, skinny cat. She—it's a she—decided to hang around our yard all the time. I don't know why she picked us. So, I started feeding her and…now Petunia is my cat. And she's not skinny anymore."

"Well. Maybe that explains it."

"Maybe. Who knows. Or maybe I just got lucky."

"Or maybe I just wised up."

"Yeah. Took you long enough."

"Well, I'm a slow learner."

And again, up on her elbow.

She said, "Tonight at the courts…I thought it would be the same thing…. I thought…he's going to keep playing basketball with the boys, acting like I'm not there."

"So, you see? You were wrong for once."

"For once."

I got up on my elbow, too, and melded with her.

In the summer night, by the willows, long ago.

When I finally walked her home—it was past one o'clock—the streets of the development were so stock-still that the world almost could have come to an end. When we reached her house, I insisted on waiting outside, worried that her mother would scream at her and she'd come running out of it again. But it was quiet.

Making my back to Renford Park Center Road, I crossed the field and passed the courts on my left. The floodlights weren't on anymore, but in the moonlight—on the side where we'd been playing—I could vaguely make out the backboard and the hoop. The whole place seemed to disclose a different self, serene and silent.

4

Rounding the former garage in our semicircular driveway, I was perturbed to see that a light was on in the breezeway. I may also have noticed subliminally that only one of the two cars was there, but I was mainly concerned about the light. I'd known my parents wouldn't like my not coming home on time, but I hadn't expected them—or one of them—to wait up for me.

What would I say? I decided to say something almost honest—that I'd met a girl, gotten wrapped up in it and lost track of the hour.

But when I entered the breezeway, it wasn't my parents who were there; it was Nellie.

Nellie was tall and almost always wore her glasses, and had a low voice. She sometimes had a querulous tone, but it was usually edged with something playful. When she took off the glasses her face looked softer, verging on pretty. She had (still does) blue eyes like Mom; straight hair like Mom, but brown instead of Mom's brownish blond; an oval face like Mom, but without the sharpness, the features a bit more gentle, refined, and reflective.

Tonight, though—sitting like a tossed sack on the little couch that was there, glasses off, robe open on her nightgown, legs thrust forward, arms folded—she looked haggard and glum, with darkness under her eyes that looked like tear tracks.

Slowly closing the door behind me, I stood looking at her uncertainly.

She said, "Do you know what time it is?"

"Uh...two?"

"Yeah, two."

She said—sitting there with her arms folded, not looking at me—"Grandpa had a stroke tonight."

I said, "What?"

"Yeah, a stroke. While you were out having fun, Steve."

"Oh boy, I guess I'm wicked. Is he OK?"

"Not really. He might die, or maybe not. Mom and Dad already left for New York City. Everyone was looking for you, Steve. You really should take other people into account."

"I suppose I should...I'm not sure I could swing it."

"You don't know how scared Mom was. She thought something happened to you, too."

"To me...? What the hell would happen to me out there?"

Now she plunged her face into her hands, sighed, and sat there.

When her face emerged again, she was looking at me with weariness, disdain, and haggardness.

She said, "Where were you?"

"I was out...I was with Connie Landry."

She said, "Connie...*Landry?*"

She was gazing straight at me.

"Yeah, something wrong with that?"

She collapsed against the backrest, her hands over her face.

Emerging again, she looked straight ahead, not at me. "Connie Landry. Do you know that she tried to kill herself?"

I said, "*What?*"

I said, "How would I not have heard about that?"

"You didn't hear about it because it's a secret."

"Then how do you know about it?"

Now she looked at me, sardonically.

"I happen to be friends with one of the people who know about it."

"Who?"

"Hmm. I'm not sure, Steve. I think maybe you'll have to join the FBI and investigate that."

She gave a deep sigh of weariness and disgust.

I said, finally, "So is he in a hospital?"

"Yeah. Grandma was terribly upset. Mom and Dad had to rush right down there."

"When…where did it happen?"

"They were at home. All of a sudden he couldn't talk, he fell down…."

"He *might* die?"

"The doctors say they don't know. He might recover, he might recover partially, he might not recover."

She said, "If he dies we have to go down there by bus for the funeral."

I said, "Damn."

I said, "What's this you were telling me about Connie?"

"What's this *you* were telling me about her?"

"I don't know. What do you want me to tell you?"

"What were you doing with her?"

I contemplated her; walked slowly past her to the steps leading down from the kitchen to the floor of the breezeway.

I sat down slowly on one of them, facing leftward to where she sat.

"I was at the courts and she showed up there. We started talking."

I said, "She had a fight with her mother. She ran out in the street. Jimmy Boynton and some guys gave her a ride to the courts."

"Yeah, her mother." Nellie sighed, dragged a tired hand across her face. "Her mother is a case."

"Yeah, sounds that way."

"So. What happened?"

"So we went for a walk. I took her out to the golf course."

She looked at me. Nellie's expression was now very rich: weariness, disdain, grief, along with a dim blue curiosity and something like amusement.

"So did you re-lose your virginity?"

I shifted my position, with an at-a-loss expression.

"First of all, you can't re-lose it. Second of all, no. She gave some ground rules. They didn't include that."

"And you obeyed the ground rules?"

"Yeah. Amazing, isn't it?"

I said, "What's this thing you're telling me?"

"What? Killing herself?"

"Yeah.... She didn't say anything about it."

"Why should she? She doesn't want people to know about it. She doesn't want *you* to know about it."

"When was it?"

She again sighed and sat back. "During the year. April, May... It was after a fight with her mother. She cut her wrist."

"Jesus Christ."

"Her mother found her and called an ambulance."

I said, "She's still fighting with her mother."

She said, "Steve, you *can't* tell anyone this. Really. You cannot tell Connie that you know this."

"OK. What am I going to do—hey, my sister spilled the beans about you?"

"A social worker was involved. She wanted to move Connie out of there to some foster family but Connie refused. She was too worried about what might happen to her mother if she was alone."

We both sat there in the stillness.

Nellie was looking at me.

"You really like Connie."

"Yeah, I guess I do."

She said, "Is it OK if I say something that you might not like to hear that much?"

"If you say something that I might not like to hear that much. Sure, why not. Go ahead."

She said, "Don't you think that…you know…Connie could be trouble for you? Someone who tried to kill herself a few months ago?"

"I'm not worried about it."

"No?"

"Nope."

"She's got a real bad situation."

"Well, I'll take it under advisement."

"She's still having fights with her mother, for God's sake."

"Well. Tough world out there."

She said, "Maybe you should just be careful."

"Well, I'll make a note of it."

We both sat there in the stillness; we both almost jumped out of our skin when the phone rang in the little foyer outside of our rooms.

Nellie sprang.

"Hello…? Hi, Mom… Yeah, he's here, he's fine. He got back about one…. He was just out with some kids and he forgot about the time. He says he's sorry…. Yeah. Where are you? How's grandpa…? That's good, Mom. I mean, it sounds like it could be a lot worse…. Yeah. Yeah… It's all right. I wasn't sleeping anyway…. OK. OK, Mom. Good night… Yeah. Any time, any time, Mom. OK. Good night."

She came back out into the breezeway, stood with her arms folded, and stared at me.

She said, "They're in a Hot Shoppes near the city. Grandpa's stable. For now."

"That's good."

She said, "So I got you off the hook. Aren't you going to thank me?"

"Thanks."

She kept staring at me.

I said, "She's coming here tomorrow."

"Who?"

"Who. Connie."

"Coming *here*?"

"Yeah. She wants to go swimming."

"We might not be here tomorrow."

"I know, so what do you want me to do. If we're not going to be here, I'll call her and say we're not going to be here."

She sighed and shook her head. "You don't waste time, do you."

"Nope."

"That's moving really fast."

"Yeah, well. I'm a fast mover."

I said, "She likes you, by the way."

"She likes *me*?"

"Yup."

"Well, that's nice."

She pondered me.

"Well. I'm going to get some sleep."

"OK."

"Good night. What's left of it."

"Good night."

She turned toward her room, and I said, "Nellie."

I said, "That friend of yours who knows about what happened with Connie. It's Jill Haverford, right?"

She gave me a sideways, sardonic look.

"Mum's the word, Steve. You can apply for a job with the FBI."

But lying in the cool dark, I couldn't sleep at all. It wasn't what was happening with my grandfather. I wasn't close with him; he was, I believed, seventy-five—to me, ancient; he'd had, as far as I knew, a good life. I wished him well, but it was partly— maybe especially—because I didn't want anything to happen to him that would make me have to go to New York City the next day.

I couldn't, though, stop thinking about Connie. Not what had happened by the pond. Not the incredible feel of her. I could only think of her cutting herself. I couldn't get blood out of my mind.

In earliest dawn I crept as quietly as I could—so as not to disturb Nellie—out of my room. In the breezeway, I thought how Louis and Greta—in the study, at the other end of the house—were emerging from the dark, their faces taking shape.

I opened the breezeway door like a bank robber, stepped out.

Though the light was still just a proposition, tentative, the birdsong was astonishingly loud. To the left was the lilac hedge, before me a short stretch of grass. It ended in, on the left, a woodshed that was behind the lilac hedge, and to the right of the woodshed, the line of trees.

The woodshed, and the trees, looked dark and somber now in the murky light. I walked out on the grass; the dew seeped through my slippers. I saw Tom step out from the woodshed where he'd been sleeping on a burlap sack, sit at its entrance and contemplate the scene.

I came to a place and stopped.

Across Kaisley Road, over the cornfield and the just-visible farmhouses, there was a reef of red light.

I felt Tom brush up against my leg. I reached down and grazed his head, said, "*Hey Tom. Hey Tom.*" He was purring.

I looked into the red light.

I said, "I love her. Nothing like that will ever happen to her again."

5

When I came back to my room I slept, but only for a few hours. At about nine o'clock—still total quiet from Nellie's room—I went to the kitchen. I wasn't hungry at all; I took a couple of cookies and a cup of coffee.

At the table, a shaft of sun streamed in and lit up the red-and-white-checked oilcloth.

I thought I should feel wonderful about Connie, but I didn't. Yes, a setback had happened—maybe—with Grandpa. But even if I had to go down to the city for a couple of days, I'd come back, and Connie would be here. Connie. *It had happened* with Connie. She might even be here today. It was wonderful. Yet I couldn't shake a glum feeling.

Tom was scratching at the back breezeway door to come in, and after removing the cookie crumbs and setting the coffee cup in the sink, I let him in; served him cat food and water in the kitchen as he pranced and purred.

I realized that—having slept so little and eaten so little—the caffeine was already causing a slight throbbing in my temples.

I thought I'd go back to my room; but on the way there, in the little foyer, I stopped.

Beside me was the small table with the phone on it, and a slim Renford Park phone book.

I picked up the phone book like a strange, dubious object. I found a Janine Landry at 41 Beechwood, and the number.

It was still too early to call; I decided to wait another hour or so.

Yet I picked up the receiver, stood there and dialed the number.

The voice that said, "Hel-lo?" could have been that of the most polite, polished receptionist.

"Hello. Can I speak to Connie?"

"Just a minute... *Connie!*"

I heard faint motion and words between them.

"Hello?"

"Connie. Hi."

"*Steve!*"

"How you doing?"

"OK. OK. Listen, I'm going up to my room, OK? Just a minute?"

"Yeah, sure."

While she was doing that I took the phone into my room, shut the door on the cord, and sat down at the edge of the bed—as far as the cord would allow. It was never comfortable holding the phone and the receiver this way, but I preferred it because it was relatively private.

I heard, "*Mom, could you hang up the phone...! Mom, could you hang up the phone...! Damn it.... Mom! Mom...! Could you hang up, please? I'm...I'm on the phone up here! Could you hang up downstairs please...?*"

Finally I heard the click.

"Hello?"

"Hello."

"Hi!"

"Hi."

"How you feeling?"

"Me? I'm feeling good. Not that great, I guess, I hardly slept. But I'm OK."

"Yeah, I didn't sleep that much either."

"A lot going on."

She laughed. "Yeah, for sure."

"Everything OK when you got back?"

"Oh, yeah… She was out cold."

"That's good. I guess. You wouldn't believe what happened when I got back."

"Oh, no."

"No, it's not what you think. A light was on in the breezeway, and I thought, oh hell, I'm screwed. Then I come in, and it's not my parents, it's my sister."

"Your *sister*?"

"Yeah. Turns out my parents weren't there. They had to run to New York City because my grandfather had a stroke."

"Oh, no."

"Yeah, they're down there now."

"Oh, I can't believe this. How's he doing?"

"Last I heard he's hanging on. He's pretty old. He might get better. The doctors don't know."

"Wait. This is…your father's father?"

"My mother's."

"Oh. She must be upset."

"Yeah, she is. If he dies…we'll have to go down there."

"Oh, wow."

"But for now—last I heard—he's hanging on. So you can still come."

"Swimming?"

"Yeah."

"Yeah, I wanted to talk about that."

I sat there, perched uncomfortably.

"Steve. I was thinking about this. I'm not sure it's a good idea if I come there today."

"You're not...why?"

She sighed. "I should have talked to you about this."

She said, "Steve, I've been through some bad things lately. I'm kind of in a fragile state."

I cleared my throat. "Fragile?"

"Yeah, it's a long story. Steve. I can't get hurt. I can't even take a chance of getting hurt. If I do, I break. And when I break, it's really not good."

"Why should you get hurt?"

"Steve. Things happen."

"You're not going to get hurt."

"Steve. Things happen in these situations. You're a guy that girls die over. Do you know that?"

"I don't know if I know it, but I'm not thinking about girls. I'm thinking about you. I want you to come here. I'm not going to do anything to hurt you. Ever. I...I want to see you."

She said, finally, "I want to too."

I sat there, the silence unbearable, but resolved not to be the next to speak.

"Steve... Can I think about this? I need time."

"I guess so."

"I'll call. OK?"

"When?"

"When. I don't know. I don't know anymore. I just...need time."

"All right, Connie. What can I say. Take your time. Take your time."

"Steve..."

"If something happens here, and we have to go down there, can I let you know? Is that OK?"

"Yes. Of course."

"OK. So, I guess it's bye for now."

"Yes. OK. Bye. For now."

I put down the receiver.

I sank my head into my tense fingers. My temples were pounding.

I put the phone back, closed the door tight, dropped forward onto the bed, holding my head.

The next thing I knew there was a harsh, persistent knocking on the door. I clutched my temples, which hurt fiercely. I was somewhere in a dark vault, not at all clear about who I was or what was happening.

The door opened.

"Steve."

"Uh?"

"Steve."

"*What.*"

"Mom called from New York City. Grandpa died."

And again: "Steve."

"OK, whaddya want me to do."

"I don't want you to do anything. Amy's mom can give us a ride to the bus station. You have to get ready. She's coming in an hour."

Again: "Steve."

"Uh."

"Steve… She's coming in an hour. We have to be packed and ready."

"Yeah, yeah."

She closed the door again. I lay there clutching my head.

December 17-20, 1975

6

It was a winter morning at Winslow College. December, the snow fresh, the sky brilliant blue, the air piercing. Having finished a class at ten, I walked along the sidewalk at one edge of the campus. I was on the way to a favorite café—across the street from the campus. I could have gone to the rathskeller, which was cheaper, but since late September of my freshman year—three years back—I'd been, by choice, mostly solitary.

It was a small private college in the little town of Winslow, a couple of hours south from where we lived, down the Hudson River and a bit north of Poughkeepsie. It wasn't a distinguished college, but my high school grades hadn't been distinguished either. With Nellie it had been different; she'd gotten a scholarship from Yale and was now, in her junior year, a star student in languages there.

The atmosphere in the café in the midmorning was pleasant; not too many customers, the usual warm smiles for me, a familiar figure. The coffee with two spoons of sugar was standard; the only question, each time, was which pastry I favored. Today I took the almond croissant; settled at my usual table by the window, looking out at the snowy street.

Since that time—that late September—I'd gone through two years of depression; in this last year it had lifted only somewhat, and I kept going to the same psychologist. I'd found him back then—luckily—through a referral service the college had. Not long after I started going to him, he'd seen a way to help me. For one thing, he'd said that, since the Jewish issue was so important to me, perhaps being with a girl who was non-Jewish would have created problems in the future. That had caught me up short—thinking that there might be something to it, that there might be a hint of solace in it. But even more significantly, he'd seen that I had a curiosity about things Jewish, and encouraged me to pursue it—and not worry about how Jews defined me, whether they "accepted" me or not. He said I should just do it for myself, that it would give me a new and positive direction. He was right; for a time it put just enough momentum in my life that I could get up in the morning, with something to look forward to; and now, when it was less crucial but still needed, I was just as engaged with it.

I was an English major, took a creative writing course in some of the semesters, and one of my activities at the café—which also boosted me—was to work on short stories. The two or three creative writing teachers I had at Winslow were, by and large, impressed by what I wrote—stories mostly taken from the high school world. Usually these narratives were downbeat, centering on a rejection by a girl. The protagonists often got drunk, but one of them, after roaming the streets of the development at night, finally comes home at dawn into a redemptive scene of dim light and birdsong.

And my other activity at the café in the mornings was what I would call my Jewish studies. They were totally independent of my coursework. Helped by the psychologist—Bob, non-Jewish—to acknowledge that I had a consuming curiosity about the subject, I bought whatever books I could find at the campus bookstore and took out others from the library. On the religious axis, I read about Hasidism, Kabbalah, a book about the Talmud, a book about the Jewish Sabbath. On the national axis, I learned from history books how the Jews had been in Israel very long ago, lost it, regained it, then lost it again—seemingly for good, before improbably returning after an astoundingly long period of wanderings. On the combined religious-national axis, I read much of the Hebrew Bible itself (I somehow felt it was too private an activity to engage in at the café, and I tried to hover over the book—the King James version—so others couldn't see it); I found a lot of it intensely engaging. Yet what stirred me most of all was the recent history—Zionism, the Holocaust, Israel, incredible, unfathomable.

All this seemed to mesh with another development. As I mentioned, along with his research into the universe at large my father took an interest in earthly affairs. In those years—the early and mid-1970s—he moved into the conservative camp. He didn't like the campus demonstrations that somehow mixed condemnations of American "imperialism" with demands for easier grading; the rise of the counterculture with its drugs; the beginnings of political correctness and the knocking of the Western heritage. And there was something else—maybe more than all those phenomena—that disturbed him: the surge of harsh criticism of Israel, much of it from the mainstream left.

On a day sometime in the autumn of my last year of high school, I was sitting at the kitchen table—probably finishing up dessert—and my father was there too, drinking coffee, puffing a cigarette, and reading the *New York Times*, which he received every day at RPI.

He pushed the paper toward me and said, "Look at this. Yesterday the Security Council condemned Israel for building a settlement—actually just for plans to build one. Today, four Israelis killed in a terrorist attack. No condemnation."

I leaned over so I could scan the report—very short—with my eyes.

I said, "Yeah, I guess they've got it in for Israel no matter what."

It began there, and it continued; he turned to me more and more on Israel matters, and I was quite responsive. Of course, I was happy he was talking with me, and I was also starting to take an interest myself. The question of whether or not I was a Jew—a person who should be concerned about Israel in particular—was of course never touched upon. His feelings about Israel and its troubles were now quite intense and—uncharacteristically for him—he had an urge to share them. He tried to do so with my mother and Nellie too, but with less success. With me he had an eager partner.

By the time I went to Winslow my father was sending me articles about Israel in the mail, and usually brought up the topic during my weekly phone conversations with him and my mother. In October 1973, during my sophomore year, with Israel embroiled in the Yom Kippur War, it reached a peak of intensity; the supposedly three-way conversations were mostly me and him talking about the war.

As for my own inner struggles, I never told either parent much about them (though they knew, of course, about Bob, since they paid for him). Yet the captivation with Israel and the Jewish dimension generally, and the channel of friendship with my father that had opened, were a raft that—along, of course, with Bob—kept me jostling forward on the rough stream.

I wasn't living a double life but at least a triple life, if not more. After the traumatic events early in my freshman year, I lost interest in socializing with my peers. The plunge into depression put me in a different universe from their gaiety, partying, booze-drinking, cannabis-smoking. That first year, living in a dorm, I had to keep deflecting the flirting girls, the invitations to parties; I was seen as mysteriously withdrawn. After that I took part in renting a different off-campus flat each year—with roommates I didn't know and didn't bother getting to know—and it was easier. I didn't, unfortunately, stop boozing myself, but I did it at night, alone in my room.

The lack of a social life, though, meant I had time for my Jewish studies, which were pretty much a secret from almost everyone but Bob. I didn't mention them to my father; I'd say, in retrospect, that the Israel-connection with him was too precious and I feared adulterating it with anything else, feared that I might lose it if I did anything to alter it in the slightest. Meanwhile I took my courses on great fiction, poetry, and drama, doing well in them, and wrote my stories, showing them to the teachers when I took creative-writing courses. There was, though, one other person, apart from Bob, who knew what had happened and how I was contending with it—Nellie. I'd talk with her when we were both home for holidays or the winter break. It was an old habit, and it stayed.

On that morning in the café—December 17, 1975—I sat by the window as the snowy world glittered in the sun. I felt relatively good, though knowing I still had the darkness in me. Coffee cup in hand, I was bearing down on *A History of Zionism* by Walter Laqueur.

That year I rented the top floor of a house with Yuan, an exchange student from China and a chemistry major, and Neil, a shy, pimply guy studying agronomics. After finishing up at the café that morning, I didn't have another class till mid-afternoon, and I went home to grab lunch and maybe some rest.

The house was on a side street, leafy in summer, now pleasantly draped with snow. I mounted the stairs; the door to our floor wasn't locked. I spied Yuan in the kitchen. I set down my knapsack, took off my coat.

Yuan came to the entrance to the kitchen.

"Hi, Steve!"

"Hey, Yuan."

"You have a call from someone."

"A call?"

"Yes."

He took a slip of paper from his pocket and peered at it very intently.

"It's from…Marcie…Dunton. She says you should call home right away."

"Call home?"

"Yes."

Marcie Dunton was my mother's best friend, a teacher at the school where she worked. I knew this wasn't something good.

Our only phone was on the wall of the kitchen; I went there. I dialed the long-distance number.

It was my mother who answered.

"Mom?"

"Stevie…"

"Mom? Is everything OK?"

She said, "Stevie…"

She said, "You wouldn't believe it. Daddy died."

"*What?*"

"Stevie…"

"What happened?"

"He was shoveling snow. With his bad lungs and his bad heart. I begged him not to. He wouldn't listen."

"What happened?"

"He fell down. It was a heart attack. The ambulance came. It was much too late. Stevie…"

"Is anyone there?"

"Marcie's here."

"Where's Nellie?"

"She's coming. Stevie…Stevie…"

"Mom, it'll be all right."

"You have to come here."

"Of course. Of course. There's a bus…I'll find out about the bus. It might not be till the afternoon."

"What will I do?"

"It'll be OK, Mom."

"How he wouldn't listen…"

The nearest bus station to our home was in the small city of Schenectady. The bus pulled in at about three o'clock. Up here, further north, the snow was higher; it was in banks along the sidewalks. The city bustled, grey and brown amid the dirty snow, the sky sullen.

They'd arranged that Amy Goldberg, Nellie's best friend, would pick me up. Amy was going to the state university in nearby Albany, studying social work, and still living at home.

She spied me the moment I entered the terminal; she ran up and hugged me.

"Steve. I'm so sorry."

"Amy, thanks for this. Really thanks."

Her car was in a parking lot beside the terminal. Amy had a narrow face, with black, long, wavy hair. At a glance it might have seemed a sober, sedate, unremarkable face; but the calm beauty grew on you. That day her coat was open on a red velour top—tight—and jeans.

"Steve," she said—turning around and peering as she backed the car out of the space—"I was so shocked. I couldn't believe it."

"Yeah," I said. "So sudden."

"So sudden…"

The car pulled out into the street—honks, congestion, annoying waits.

I said, "I guess he didn't take care of himself. But…I wasn't at all prepared for something like this."

"You can't prepare yourself for something like this, Steve."

"How's my mother?"

"You know what, Steve? She's going to be all right. Because she's a tough person."

"Nellie's there?"

"Nellie's there. Poor Nellie. She's so wonderful with your mom. I can't believe all this is happening."

There were snowbanks, too, beside the part of our driveway where the two cars were parked—and now a third, Amy's. (It turned out it was Marcie's son who had shoveled it.) As we got out of the car, I looked at the house. He was not in it. He never would be again.

My mother and Nellie almost ran down the steps to us in the breezeway. They looked—for a moment—disconcertingly similar, haggard and aged. They hugged me with something like desperation. Tom, too, ran to me; rubbed my legs blissfully, purring.

"Oh, Stevie," my mother said. "I'm so, so glad you're here."

"Steve, you probably want coffee or something," said Nellie.

"Yeah, coffee would be good."

"I'll get it," Amy said. "You people…*please* take it easy. I'll get it."

As we sat at the table—leaving the chair at the head of the table, my father's, empty—Amy bustled in the kitchen. I noticed that something in me was monitoring Amy—tracking her every move.

My mother and Nellie were sitting across from me. They looked a bit different from each other now. My mother, wan and stricken; Nellie—her glasses off—with dull eyes, as if she'd awoken from a gloomy sleep.

"What am I supposed to do without him?" my mother said.

"*Mom*," said Nellie. "You can't worry about that now. It just makes it worse when you think like that."

As Amy came around the partition—a steaming coffee cup in one hand, a tray of cookies and nuts in the other—her eyes met mine. I thought, *This is insane.*

I said, "Thanks, Amy."

"*Don't* mention it."

She set the cup beside me, set the tray in the middle of the table, sat down beside me. My father's chair remained empty.

"Stevie," my mother said.

"So you got here faster than me," I said to Nellie.

"Yeah. Mom was able to reach me just as I was getting up."

"I was at some café. Didn't get home till eleven or something."

My mother started crying. Nellie said "*Mom*" and put her arm around her.

"Stevie," my mother said. "He was so proud of you."

"Of *me*?" Now I felt like crying—but didn't, of course.

She gazed at me through her tears. "He was so happy to be able to talk about Israel with you."

"Oh. Yeah...I was happy too."

"You know what he said? Just yesterday...just yesterday..."

"Mom," Nellie said.

"He said he wanted us to go there. All of us. He wanted all of us to take a trip there."

"Really?" I said. "To Israel?"

"Amy was there," Nellie said, smiling—dully—at Amy.

"Oh, you were there?" I said, turning to Amy—awkwardly; there was an oblique mutual glance.

"Yeah. I was a kibbutz volunteer," she said, looking from me to Nellie, to my mother. "I was, let's see...fifteen."

"Oh yeah, I remember that now," I said. "How was that?"

"Was nice. I picked a lot of grapes. It was up in the Galilee, really beautiful up there."

"And you learned some Hebrew," Nellie said.

"Hebrew?" I said—not really looking at Amy this time. "What you can say in Hebrew?"

"Well," she said. "*Boker tov.* That means 'good morning.'"

"Good morning," said my mother. "It wasn't a good morning...."

"Mom," said Nellie.

7

The next morning I drove one of the cars to the shopping center to buy food. Many people would be visiting today—colleagues of my father's, friends. The funeral was the next day. It turned out that the rabbi of the synagogue Amy's parents went to in Schenectady, a Conservative rabbi, was taking care of things. He hadn't, of course, known my father at all, and he'd requested to talk about him this evening with my mother, Nellie, and me to gather information for his eulogy.

As I drove, I was aware that something, after three years, had changed: I didn't have the terror of seeing Connie somewhere. There was still a fear, but it was somewhat mixed with curiosity. I knew that it wasn't my father's death—huge and numbing as it was—that had caused the change. It was Amy.

I was passing the courts on the left. They were covered with snow; one of the basketball hoops, the one farther from the clubhouse, no longer had its net, but from the one closer to the pool the net still hung, white in the blue, beckoning as if one could possibly play now in the snow. That, too—the basketball court—had been painful to see in these years. Now, though, it wasn't; the feeling was more like nostalgia mixed with wonder. I even thought of driving down to the golf course, getting out of the car and walking to the pond. But what would be the point in the winter?

The day was something of a nightmare—a succession of visitors, always bearing a large cake. My mother, as if she didn't have enough trouble, had to play the hostess—pale and befuddled. Nellie, of course, shielded her when she was at her side, but sometimes she had to leave her so she could make coffee and the like. I did my best to field the hopeless, awkward questions; help endure the even more hopeless silences. I didn't know how to converse with physics professors and their wives.

In the afternoon, though—having finished her classes and come back from Albany—Amy showed up. She simply took over, relieving much of the burden on the three of us; she even, in between her other tasks, talked with the people much more capably than we could. What had happened between me and her was abrupt, mutual, and huge. I loved how efficient and selfless she was; her soft, composed voice; her shape. Now, when our eyes met, there was something like amusement in hers.

In the evening I lay down on my bed, the light off. I'd slept little since "it" had happened; now I went in and out of a dozing state. In one of those states, I was in a rowboat with my father on a lake. He said, as he rowed, "This place is very old."

There was a knock on the door.

"Yeah?"

It opened slightly; Nellie said, "Steve."

"Yeah."

"Your turn. Rabbi Jack would like to talk with you."

"OK."

Rabbi Jack Sperber was in the living room, sitting in a chair across the coffee table from the couch. When I entered he rose up to greet me. He wore a black skullcap, but other than that he could have been an up-and-coming young athlete—sandy hair, a genial and youthful face, a strong and springy build.

"Steve!" he said, extending a hand. "Pleased to meet you. I'm Rabbi Jack."

"Hi," I said as I shook his hand. "Thanks...thanks for coming."

It was past nine; he'd already talked with my mother and Nellie. I sat down on the couch; he, back in the chair, looked at me as if talking with me was a treat he'd been waiting for.

"How you feeling, Steve?"

"Oh, boy," I said, rubbing my eyes with my hand. "It's...overwhelming."

"It's a shock, isn't it?"

"Yeah... I feel like...part of me doesn't even understand what's happened."

"It takes time to process a shock."

"Yeah."

He said, "You're at Winslow College, Steve?"

"Yeah... I was just at a café...yesterday...and I came home, and one of my roommates says, there's a call for you.... Yesterday. I can't believe it was yesterday."

"The time goes real slow?"

"Yeah..."

"What can you tell me about your father, Steve?"

"Well," I said. "He didn't talk much, and I didn't know that much about him."

"Yes," he said. He was nodding—implying this wasn't the first time he'd heard that.

"When we'd stay at a lake in the Adirondacks…it was better. Had more interaction with him. It was only for about two weeks…but…it was the only time he wasn't constantly working."

"So it was like an opportunity?"

"Yeah. He'd play chess with me…and we'd go for rowboat rides."

"And what was that like, those interactions?"

I sighed. "It was really nice…. My father…he was a solid person. There was something about…just having him around, just having him in the house. You knew you could count on him, even though he was so quiet."

I said, "My sister says he was like that, so quiet, because of those traumas in his past. I don't know if that's true. But she's not mad at him. My sister's amazing that way."

"You were mad at him?"

I sat quiet, aware that something inward had been touched.

I said, "Yeah, it would have been nice if he'd done more with me, more than two weeks a year."

Rabbi Jack contemplated me.

I said, "Is it true that if only your father's Jewish, and not your mother, then you're not considered a Jew?"

He kept contemplating me, as if he wasn't going to answer; then said, "Yes. In Jewish law a Jew is someone who's born to a Jewish mother or who converts to Judaism."

"Yeah. I found that out when I was eleven. I was pretty amazed."

"Oh? Why was that?"

"Well, up until then I assumed I was a Jew. I thought if my father was, so I was. I identified with it. Even though I knew almost nothing about it."

I said, "Also…you know, with his parents, and what happened to them, and all that."

I glanced at him. His look, and a small nod, conveyed that he knew what I was referring to.

"So these last few years… It's a long story. I've been reading about the Jewish side of things. I'm an English major, so I've been reading about it on my own."

"And what have you learned?"

"What have I learned…. A lot. I've learned about the religion. I've been reading the Bible, and history books, and a lot of things. I find the Israel story the most fascinating. How people thought it was a crazy idea. How Herzl and people like him insisted that you could get something back even when it seemed so impossibly lost…."

I said, "That was what got better with my father these last few years. He was always pretty political, but he got really intense about Israel. So…we'd talk about that. There was more of a friendship between us. It was all centered on Israel."

He said, "Have you thought about converting to Judaism?"

"Thought about it, yeah… I don't know. Circumcision…"

"At your age it's done under anesthetic. Usually no more than mildly painful afterward."

"Yeah, but…I'm not really a religious person. Not formally anyway. Seems like it would be hypocritical—going through all the religious part."

"You could see it as a learning experience. Once you've converted, you don't necessarily have to be observant. Though you might—you might—see it differently by then."

I said, "If I wanted to move to Israel—now, without converting—would I be able to?"

"Yes, as someone with a Jewish parent, you would. You might have trouble with the rabbinate, though—getting married, that kind of thing."

He said, "Is that something you're thinking about?"

"Yes. I've been thinking about it."

I sat still.

"Steve, is there anything else you want to say about your father?"

I waited.

"Yes. He was quiet, but when he wanted to talk, he really knew how to. It was really nice. He gave you the feeling that he liked and respected you.... He had his contradictions, I guess."

He was looking at me intently.

"An unusual person?"

"Yes, I'd say so."

"He left quite an impression. That much I can see."

"Yes, a big impression. One way or another. A big impression for someone so quiet."

We sat, quiet.

"Steve," he said, "it's been great talking with you. Great talking with all three of you. I'm inspired to write this eulogy. I hope I'll do a good enough job."

What struck me most at the funeral was that Rabbi Jack—with his veneer of a regular American guy—was able to sing old Hebrew chants with such power and authority. It was the first time I'd ever been in a synagogue. Rabbi Jack stood above a closed coffin that had my father in it; his eulogy skillfully interwove what my mother, Nellie, and I had told him. In the evening my mother's sister, Katie, had flown in from Seattle with her husband, Len, and one of their two sons, Scott. Now we stood in the front row: Scott, Len, Katie, my mother, Nellie, me, Amy, Amy's mother, father, brother, and sister. I was very bodily aware of Amy and constantly wanted to brush her hand. It seemed way too much to be happening to a person at once.

At the cemetery, I learned of the traditional Jewish custom where male relatives of the deceased person shovel dirt onto the coffin after it's been lowered. I did it with Scott and Uncle Len, all of us grim-faced. I wasn't sure if, as non-Jews, we were really qualified to do this, but I was the only real male relative and they were the closest to being relatives. Just behind us my mother and Nellie—and Amy, and others—were crying buckets. Yet in the midst of it Rabbi Jack sang a Hebrew song—"Ya'aseh Shalom" (He Will Make Peace)—that, even without understanding the words except the ones I could pick up ("Shalom," "Yisrael"), stirred deep feelings.

The funeral was on a Friday, and of course Nellie and I were able to stay for the weekend before taking buses back to our schools early Monday morning.

On Saturday afternoon I found myself in an ice cream parlor, sitting across a table from Amy. It was—unfortunately for my mother, for us—the most hectic day yet in our house. Rabbi Jack, and Amy, had told us about the Jewish practice of the *shiva*, the seven days of mourning that are a kind of open house for visitors to make condolence calls; but on that Saturday it was like that anyway. Katie, Len, and Scott were there, and Marcie and her husband, and Amy and her parents, and many others. (As for my grandmother, she'd died a couple of years after my grandfather.) When, about two o'clock, my mother asked me to drive down to the supermarket, I had no trouble assenting. But as I went into my room for my coat, I had an idea.

I found Amy in the living room, fortunately sitting in a chair and not with others on the couch. The din was so loud that I had to kneel down so she could hear me.

"Amy, I have to go down to PriceRight. Want to come? There's a Stewart's there, we could take a break from this."

"A break from this. Yeah, I think I could go for that."

As we passed through the breezeway, Nellie was standing there with some people.

"Steve," she said. "Got company for your grocery run?"

"Yup."

"Be good, kids."

Now she sat across from me, a steaming cup of coffee in front of each of us. I had always thought of her—if at all—as a nice-looking girl who was Nellie's friend. Now, in a maroon sweater, with her soft, dark, bright eyes, she seemed to me stunningly beautiful.

"Oh, boy…" I said.

"Steve, are you holding up under this?"

"More or less…"

I said, "I don't know what's going to be with my mother."

"You guys have to leave Monday."

"Yeah… My aunt says she can get time off work and stay with her for a few days."

"My parents and I are here. I told her that. She really shouldn't hesitate."

"What's your father do, Amy?"

"My dad? He's a podiatrist."

"And your mother?"

"My mom's an intensive-care nurse at Ellis in Schenectady."

"Oh. So they're both…care providers."

"I don't know. Is a podiatrist a care provider?"

"He provides care to feet."

She laughed.

"Yeah, and they need a lot of it. Believe me."

"Did they care for you?"

She stared at me.

"*What?*"

"Did your parents provide care to you?"

"To *me*."

She said, "Overall…I would say yes. I'm still living there, after all."

"Yeah, why did you do that?"

"My mom really begged me to. Didn't want me to go off to school. And also…I don't know…living in a dorm with a bunch of other kids, doing crazy stuff all the time…it didn't appeal to me that much. I didn't really see the point."

"Yeah, there's truth to that. There isn't much point."

She said, "So how is it for you down there in Winslow?"

I looked slowly into her eyes. "I have a feeling you're asking a question that you already know a lot of the answers to."

She laughed again—it was beautiful how she did it.

"Yes. I will plead guilty to that."

She said, "I wish I could have a friendship with my siblings—with either of them—like you and Nellie have."

"Your brother…he's still in school?"

"He's in twelfth. He's kind of a problem."

I thought she didn't want to say any more about it, but she said, "He's going with these kids who smoke grass. Causing my parents *tsuris*. He sees me as…" she raised her hands and dropped them. "Hopelessly square. Not worth talking to."

"*Tsuris*. What's that?"

"I think it's Yiddish. It means…troubles, problems. My father says it a lot. My *tsuris*, my *tsuris*."

"What about your sister?"

"Rina? She's thirteen now. She's cute. She's starting with…the rebellion. Withdrawn… That's what worries me. When Sammy—my brother—started with it, he was fifteen. Rina's thirteen, and she's starting already. I don't know what will be with her."

"Oh, boy… *Tsuris*."

"*Tsuris*."

She raised her eyes to mine, with a different light in them.

"And you," she said, "have had your share of *tsuris*."

"Yes," I said. "And you know quite a lot about it."

"Yes," she said. "But it's not the same as hearing it from the source."

"And what would you like to hear about it from the source?"

"Well. I would like to hear about the business with Connie Landry."

We both fell silent.

I glanced at my watch. I knew that we were taking too long, that my mother was wondering where we were, that we should go into the supermarket so I could buy the things and go back home.

I said, "That interests you?"

"Yeah, Steve, it does."

We fell silent again.

I said, "Amy, these last few days…I don't know, it's been crazy."

I wanted to follow that up by looking into her eyes; but I couldn't.

I said, "Let's see. Connie. It started in the summer...when we were both going into eleventh. There was trouble at first, but...it took off."

She said, "It took off?"

"Yeah. It got really intense. I don't know.... I got my license, and we went all kinds of places together. Lake George, Cape Cod. It was..." I raised my hands and dropped them. "It was something."

I was aware of her looking at me, but I still wasn't looking at her.

"So, it turned out I was going to Winslow, she was going to Oneonta."

Amy nodded.

"We decided...I mean, we didn't really have to decide, we agreed easily...that we would be faithful to each other."

I said, "You know what you said about life in the dorms, kids doing crazy stuff?"

She sat very still, looking at me—almost like Bob.

I dropped my forehead into my fingers. "I was really in love with Connie. Really in love. I had *no intention* of doing what I did. No intention..."

She said, finally, "What happened?"

"Aa..."

I said, "There was a girl on my floor. Sheila. Considered a sexpot...the sexpot of the whole college."

I said, "What can I say. There was a party. Kids sitting in a circle passing joints around. She sat next to me. She kept pressing into me."

I said, "Amy, I was on a drug. I was high on a drug."

Without looking directly at her, I could see that—reacting to my pain—one of her eyes was tearing.

"I go back to my room afterward. I still had no intention of doing anything. She walks right in. She doesn't knock on the door. She wasn't wearing much."

I said, "There was nothing whatsoever with Sheila after that stupid night. I didn't want there to be."

She said, "Steve, if this is too much to go into now, after all that's—"

"No, it's all right, it's all right."

I said, "I thought about it…I realized I didn't want to have a secret from Connie, I didn't want to lie to her the rest of my life. You may think it's incredible, but we assumed that we'd be together the rest of our lives. So…I decided to tell her."

I said, "I thought she'd forgive me."

I said, "I don't know how much you know about Connie. She's a great person, but she's had it really rough. You can't… you can't take a chance with her."

I said, "So, when I told her, it was totally over between us. Totally over."

I said, "I was totally, totally stunned. I've been going to a shrink for three years to get over it."

I finally lifted my eyes to hers.

I said, "So have I invalidated myself?"

Her expression—both eyes moist—was deep and complex.

She said, "Steve, it's not that you were unfaithful to her…. Crazy kids in a dorm."

She said, "It's that you're still in love with Connie."

I said, "I'm coming out of it now. I can come out of it now."

July 21, 1982

8

By late afternoon the sun relented and I could open the sliding door to the balcony. I stepped out there. Our apartment—on the third and top story—looked out on a stretch of grass and a small pond. The pond water now appeared sedate and glassy, reflecting the pines on the other shore.

I'd been working most of the day. In the morning, on my novel; in the afternoon, on someone else's book, which I was editing. I was doing freelance copyediting for a technical publisher in New York City; the son of an old colleague of my father worked there. It wasn't too much money, not enough to get by on; Amy had a fulltime job as a social worker at Albany Memorial Hospital. I saw my more significant work as the novel. I'd been writing and rewriting it for three years; I hoped that—when it was finally ready—it could put us in a different financial bracket if it could clear the hurdles and reach a market.

It was 1982. I'd finished my MA in English at Winslow in 1978 (I stayed there, didn't transfer—still needed Bob); Amy had finished her MA in social work, at Albany, in 1979. After renting a place together in Albany for a year, we'd gotten married that summer. At that time my mother was still alone, Nellie was embarking on her PhD at Yale, and we'd moved to Tillendale Apartments, a low-rise luxury complex about a mile from our old house where my mother still lived. I was concerned that the monthly rent was beyond our means, but my mother said not to worry about it, and indeed she willingly chipped in when we fell short. Soon after we moved there, though, she'd met Ed Reiden, a very nice guy, a widower, and an electrochemist at General Electric, and now they were a happily remarried couple living in Ed's house in Schenectady.

I went to the kitchen. I put ice in a tumbler, poured some Johnny Walker on the ice. I shuffled the ice. I took a sip, sighed.

It was just about five o'clock; back in the living room I turned the TV on, plopped down on the couch.

> Israeli artillery pounded alleged PLO positions in Beirut for a third straight day today as casualties mounted. In an official statement, Israeli prime minister Menachem Begin said: "We do not covet a single inch of Lebanese territory. The sole aim of Operation Peace for Galilee is to put a stop to terrorist bombardment of our northern towns and villages and enable the residents of northern Israel to lead normal lives again. As soon as the PLO is defeated and if adequate security arrangements can be put in place, we hope to withdraw all our forces from Lebanese soil."

> Meanwhile British Labour Member of Parliament Oswald Braddock referred to the Israeli barrage on Beirut as an "appalling atrocity" and called for an urgent meeting of the United Nations Security Council to address the issue.

> U.S. defense secretary Caspar Weinberger, in a Pentagon briefing, said: "The United States recognizes

Israel's right to self-defense and to respond to the shelling of northern Israel. However, we call upon the Israeli government and armed forces to exercise maximal restraint, and we call upon both sides to seek a peaceful resolution to the conflict."

I got up, stepped over, flicked the TV off.

I lay back down on the couch, perching the tumbler on my stomach.

I said, "Fuckers."

After a while I heard Amy in the hall outside, approaching the door.

As she opened the door and came in, I said, "Hi, sweetie."

She glanced over at me, closed the door behind her.

She said, eyes fixed on the tumbler, "You're starting with that already?"

I said, "I've been working all day."

"Yeah, tell me about it.... I have to get out of these fucking clothes."

She went to our bedroom. When she came out she was wearing shorts and a tank top.

She went to the kitchen, poured herself a glass of something, gulped it down. She went to a chair facing me, slumped into it, arms folded and legs thrust out.

"Rough day there, Steve?"

"Sweetie, I want to kiss you. Actually a few times."

"Don't give me that now Steve, OK?"

I was still lying on my back, balancing the tumbler on my stomach.

I said, "Amy, I don't know why you think editing a badly written book about risk management in industrial planning isn't work."

"Yeah, and writing stories about your old lover girl."

I sighed. "Oh, boy…"

I said, "Amy, I'd never have thought it would be so hard making clear to a person like you what a fiction writer is. Yes, I draw from my own life. I'm sorry. I can't write historical novels about ancient Carthage. I'm not cut out for it."

"Steve, if I have to spend another eight hours like that, running from floor to floor of that goddamn hospital, dealing with goddamn insane people…."

Elaborately, carefully, I set the tumbler on the coffee table, sat up. I took a sip, faced Amy.

She was sitting there, hunched into herself.

"OK. Why don't you look for better work in the field. Working with families or something like that."

"You know the answer, Steve. It's because you keep us in limbo all the time. All the time talking about the big move to the Holy Land, right? So how the hell am I supposed to plan anything for my life?"

I sat still.

"I thought you were opposed to that."

"Yeah, maybe I am. Do I have a choice? Here I am, a bona fide, certified Jew, and I actually feel attached to the country I grew up in. Actually feel attached to my family. What a crime."

"Amy, sweetie, this is your country only if you want to close your ears and close your eyes. The Israelis are fighting for their lives. Our government is…ripping into them. Nobody cares about a bunch of Jews out there. You're either with them or not with them."

"Yeah, Steve, I live with you, I see your passion about it, and you know what? It seeps in. It seeps even if you don't want it to seep in. And meanwhile, if it's so important to you, why do you keep us in limbo about everything? When do you finish the book, and when does it become a great bestseller? When do you get a normal job? I could even think about having a kid, but I can't, because I don't know where I am, I don't know where I live, I don't know what I'm doing, I don't know anything…."

She cried.

"Sweetie…"

"Steve, don't give it to me."

I sighed. I stood up, walked with the drink to the edge of the balcony.

The pond looked placid. There were people beside it now—a couple of fishermen, kids playing.

I said, looking out at the pond, "I want to finish the book first, and see if it gets someplace. That can give us more of a basis to move there. I realize that I'm living in artistic time, and it's not simple. I can't predict how long things will take. I can't predict when a chapter will get straightened out, or how long the whole thing will take. It's artistic time…it's not the same as practical time. I guess it's nerve-wracking."

She said, "Steve, I want to rest now, OK? You go about your business. I'm sorry, I'm not feeling social. The social worker is not feeling social. I just…want to get some rest. I'm sorry I'm like this. It's just been a day like that, the whole day's been like that."

I said, "OK."

Toward nightfall, dusky grey outside, I sat at the desk of my study, which was just off the living room. On the desk was a cassette player; it was playing a cassette-tape Hebrew course, which asked me questions and gave me blanks to fill in. I complied in a low voice. It was an intermediate course, which I'd ordered after conquering the beginner course. I'd tried to get Amy to take the courses, too; she always said she'd get around to it, but she didn't.

I took another sip from the tumbler of scotch beside me—it was the third; I sighed, flicked off the cassette player. I turned off the lamp.

To my left on the desk was a tall stack of pages—it was the novel I was working on.

Left of the desk, through the screen, came the sounds of the late dusk—crickets; cooing and trilling noises from the pond.

The stack of pages looked neat and solid—more than it actually was. I knew that some of the chapters were still in provisional, unsatisfactory states; that in some cases there were two or even three versions of the same chapter one upon the other; that the bottom of the stack was not really the bottom, because the concluding chapter or two were still lacking.

In the pages, Ken and Stacy lived—high school kids, in love. Stacy, from a problematic background, was unstable; she'd tried suicide once, and when things went badly between them, Ken was gripped by anxiety that she'd try it—maybe even succeed—again. His life was a rollercoaster of huge highs and unbearable lows.

It hadn't, actually, been that way with Connie. After we'd started, she'd mostly been on an even keel—cheerful, funny, glowing. There were lows when she had a fight with her mother, but they didn't last too long; what was happening was too wonderful for her.

But where was the story, the novel, in that—a youthful, innocent, blissful romance? For a story there had to be trouble; so I kept Stacy in a no-man's-land of fluctuation, with an ever-present risk of her plunging dangerously deep. Yet where did such a story lead, how could it end? If she got over her volatility, and they emerged in happiness, it was saccharine; if worse came to worst and she put an end to herself, it might be effectively tragic, but how many people would want to *buy* such a terrible story? I'd even toyed with the idea that *Ken*—unable to bear the tension and anxiety of his life any longer—would be the one to do away with himself; but, again, what could that give presumptive readers except a painful jolt?

Sitting there in the dimness, I looked at the tall, dark stack.

Wasn't Amy right?

Wasn't this novel—irresolvable, going in circles for three years—really just a world, an island, where I could keep being with "Stacy"?

I sat on the balcony, drinking a fourth scotch. It was night. The pond kept making its outlandish noises. I could hear Amy taking a shower.

After a while she came and stood at the edge of the balcony, looking at me.

I said, "Sweetie, aren't you going to eat something?"

"I might get to it…. You?"

"It's OK. I've been taking stuff from the kitchen."

"Yeah. Taking stuff. I can see."

She pulled up a chair and sat in it—not too far from me, but not too close.

"Steve, what is it with the scotch? After what happened with your father, I can't understand how you can do this."

"My father was a chain smoker. Isn't that a bit worse?"

"Maybe worse, but what you're doing really isn't good. And it's really getting more and more extreme."

I sighed.

"You were right before. The book's putting me under pressure. It's putting us under pressure. I think I'm going to put it aside for a while. Then we can start planning our *aliyah*" (a move to Israel).

"I wish I could say that makes me happy."

I sighed again; drank the scotch.

She said, after a while, "How romantic... A summer night... A pond..."

"Amy, I'm sorry I told you things about my past. I thought we were supposed to be open with each other. I'm sorry I told you things about my romantic past."

"Oh, I don't have a problem with things about your romantic past. I have a problem when it's the present."

I sighed.

I said, "I want to have Jewish children with you in the Land of Israel."

She sat still for a while.

She said, "Just think. Bona fide, fully authorized Jewish kids. You couldn't have done *that* with the other one. That might at least console you."

"I don't need to be consoled."

"Yeah, and what exactly am I supposed to do there? What is an English-speaking social worker supposed to do there? I'll end up wiping off tables."

"First of all, there are organizations there for English-speaking immigrants, and they need social workers. Second of all, you can learn Hebrew, but you don't want to."

"If I learn Hebrew it will be with human beings, not with a cassette."

"The cassette consists of recordings of human beings."

We both sat silently. The stars were splayed out over the pond.

I said, "Life is actually good there. Not like what you see on TV. It's considered a great place for raising kids. Family life is really strong."

"Yeah, especially when your family is there."

"*Our* family will be there. Your parents, and my mother, will have no problem hopping over there on a jet to visit us as much as they want to."

"And my brother and sister? How are they supposed to get there?"

"They'll manage."

"Will they, Steve? My brother has a job selling vacuum cleaners now."

"So we'll visit them."

"Yeah? We're going to swing that? Where are *we* going to get the money for that?"

"Oh, boy..."

I said, "You loved it when you were there."

"Oh, when I was there. As a kid. Picking grapes on a kibbutz, with Israeli guys gawking at me. Sure, anybody'd love that. Steve, I have nothing against Israel. I'm pro-Israel. I'm glad it's there. I think it's great. I think it can survive without me, though."

"That's where you're wrong. They need us. They need every one of us."

"And what are you going to do there, Steve? Start working on your book again?"

"And why should that bother you?"

"You know why it bothers me."

I said, "Yes, I'm nostalgic about the past. Maybe to a fault. It's not uncommon among writers."

I said, "Look, it had to do with how suddenly it ended. The trauma of it... The only thing I could compare it to was when my father died. The shock. But then I said…he was a chain smoker, he didn't take care of himself, what did you expect. With this…boom. It was gone. I don't know, it shook me up. I'm sorry."

"It's not just that."

She said, "It's not just how it ended."

I said, "What I care about is you, me, and the future."

She said, "I don't want to leave my family."

She started crying.

I moved my chair—drunkenly—over to hers; I put my arm around her. She didn't resist or respond.

"Amy…"

September 14, 1987

9

Toward dusk we trooped back down from the firing range, dusty and sweaty; it was September and had been burning hot all day. Around us were the tawny hills of Samaria, Arab villages nestled against them with rectangular houses and minarets. It had been another day of basic training; it still wasn't over since I had guard duty in the evening. Now we could go back to our row of tents, take showers, head off to the dining hall.

Ricardo drew up beside me.

"Steven," he said. "We have gate duty tonight at eight."

"I know," I said. "We can hijack a jeep and get out of here."

He laughed.

"Steven," he said. "We will get through this. It's because we have no choice. It's something I've learned here—when you have no choice, you survive. It's almost scary how much strength you have. But you do have it."

"I know, Ricardo. There were times when I thought I'd tell him, 'Look, I'm thirty-three years old and I cannot do this. I can't do it.' And yet—I did it. I might have been in unbearable pain, like that time he made us run up the hill over and over again. And yet, I did it. It makes me think I can do just about anything. What an awful thought."

He laughed. We were turning into the dusty path along which our tents stood.

"Steven," he said. "These NCOs. They have no way to make themselves feel important but to scream at us and make us suffer. What can we do."

It was 1987. We'd moved to Israel (made *aliyah*) exactly three years ago—in September 1984. A year before that our son Lior (named after my father's father) had been born. As was the practice in those days, we'd started out in an immigrant absorption center. It was in the town of Mevaseret Zion, a few miles west of Jerusalem. You lived in a tiny, almost-free apartment and took an intensive Hebrew course five hours a day, with free care for kids too young to go to the nearby school. For me, at least, the charm of being there—in a Hebrew environment, in the Land—was huge. I hadn't converted to Judaism; as someone who had had a Jewish parent, and was married to a Jew, I was doubly qualified to immigrate.

In the spring we'd bought, and moved into, a small apartment in Maale Adumim, a community slightly east of Jerusalem—technically a settlement because it was on land Jordan had once occupied for nineteen years. We'd picked the Jerusalem area because I had a contact—through the guy at the technical publisher—in the higher administrative echelons of Hebrew University, which is in Jerusalem. This person, the contact, said she could find me freelance editorial work.

In fact, she did; by now I had something of a name in the university's political and international relations departments. They fed me a steady flow of articles and books to edit—sometimes in very raw form, in woeful English written by non–native English speakers. So the work could be grueling, but it added up to decent earnings by the Israeli standards of the time.

Amy, alas, had fared less well. It turned out that organizations to help English-speaking immigrants *did* engage social workers—but on a volunteer basis, and we needed the second income. She progressed decently in Hebrew, but still could hardly do social work in it. So she was working at a Steimatzky's bookstore in downtown Jerusalem—saying "*Efshar la'azor?*" to native-Israeli customers and "Can I help you?" to others, finding books for them, or sometimes just doing cash-register duty. I told her that eventually she'd be able to work in her field; but I wasn't really sure of it.

Further complicating life was the fact that Lior turned out to be a handful—very sweet and affectionate, also very wild. Fortunately the *metaplot*—women who ran private day-care services in their homes—were gracious about taking him on and couldn't help liking him. But it added stress to our lives.

Meanwhile I hadn't resumed work on my novel. Of course, I'd taken it with me; but it was in a drawer. Why did I shy away from it? For one thing, I was too busy; there was too much going on. But, for another, it was a concession to Amy. She'd made *aliyah* with me, an idea she'd never have had by herself and did not delight in. She did respond—as a Jew and as a person—positively to aspects of Israel: the soulful quality of many of the people; the way the Jewish holidays were colorful events for the whole country; the beauty of Jerusalem, and of the Judean Desert beside it where we now lived; the challenge and fun of learning a new language. But, on the other hand, her fears seemed to be materializing. She wasn't working in her field but in a bookstore. Her parents had already visited us three times—in the summers of '85, '86, and '87—but she hadn't seen her brother or sister since the move. My mother and Ed, too, had visited us three times; but Nellie—my sister, Amy's best friend—was now married with two little kids and had managed it only once. It was, of course, still some years before people had personal email, and more years yet before Skype and the like.

In light of all that, a firm inner voice told me not to resume working on the book. We both knew what—among other things—it meant: spending considerable parts of each day (not only when writing, but also when thinking about the writing) in a fantasy world where "Stacy" played a lead role. It was far from sure that—even if I did resume writing it and finished it—it could get published, let alone sell. All the more reason not to subject Amy to that, too, on top of everything else.

I did, however, write. It started while we were still in the absorption center. I penned an article on the "*aliyah* experience"; I mailed it to an American Jewish magazine. Maybe three weeks later I received a reply that they were planning to run it. After we moved to Maale Adumim, I wrote more pieces in that vein—an immigrant's experiences in Israel—and sent them to the same and other American Jewish magazines. It was nice to do; they got published; there was money in it—not huge sums but it helped. And I tried another tack—I sent an opinion piece to the *Jerusalem Post*, then Israel's only English-language daily. The article argued that, despite the talk in some circles about the PLO (Palestine Liberation Organization) having changed and being ready for peace with Israel, their actual words and behavior proved otherwise. This time, instead of hearing from the *Post*, I just opened it a couple of days later—and there was my article on the op-ed page, its title and my name in bold print. When I called the op-ed editor he assured me I'd get paid, and asked me to send more pieces. So I added opinion articles, too, to the mix of things I did.

By the spring and summer of 1987, Shalav Bet—Level B—was impending. In those days male immigrants to Israel aged about 25 to 35 had to do Shalav Bet: two months of basic military training, scaled to guys of an older age than the young recruits, followed by two more months of more specific training (in my case it was for the artillery corps); after that you were assigned to a reserve unit and did reserve duty like other Israelis. During Shalav Bet you could go home every weekend, and if you told them that the whole thing was too difficult and you and your family couldn't handle it, you could get out of it pretty easily.

That, in any case, was what Amy asked me to do. I said it was simply too essential an aspect of *aliyah* and I couldn't forgo it (looking back, I feel that even more strongly). Our neighbors in Maale Adumim were a native-Israeli couple a few years younger than us; Ofer and Etti, who had two kids around Lior's age, became our friends and were enthused to help us out. If you kept an eye on them, Lior and the two kids played together happily. I emphasized to Amy that, while I was away in Shalav Bet, Ofer, Etti, and their kids would be there; Amy could take Lior over there to play, and indeed Ofer and Etti helped her a lot. Still, Amy had to drive into Jerusalem to the bookstore each day, come back in the afternoon and pick Lior up from the nursery school (he'd moved on to it from *metaplot*), then deal with him—bouncy and wild—by herself at least part of the time. Not easy.

After supper in the mess hall, I had a couple of hours before guard duty—but there was another mission: calling Amy. From that place it was always a trial. It was still a few years before cell phones came to Israel. You called from an old-style phone in a booth, next to the huts where the officers and their assistants did their paperwork. They'd arranged that we could make our calls for free, but you had to wait in line; there was always, in the scant time they gave us, a throng. When your turn came, it was understood that you had only a couple of minutes; more than that and people—irate after a grueling day—started to carp at you.

It was already dark. When my turn came, able to see the phone only dimly in light from one of the officers' huts, I dialed as hastily as I could.

"Hello?"

"Amy, sweetie, hi."

"Hi."

"What's doing?"

"Not too well."

"No?"

"Lior threw two plates today."

"What?"

"It was after *gan*.[1] He was in a terrible mood as usual. I was on the phone with Etti. He got mad because I dared to keep talking to her. He went into the kitchen. He took two plates out of the drainer and smashed them on the floor."

"Oy, oy, oy…"

"I go in there, they're lying there in pieces."

"Oh, boy…"

"Steve, can you get out again on Thursday?"

"On Thursday? Again…? I don't know. Everybody looks over everybody else's shoulder here."

She said nothing.

---

[1] Nursery school or kindergarten.

"I don't know, Amy. People say, why does he get to get out every Thursday? I can't explain to the whole platoon that I have a hyperactive son. It's a matter of the morale of the platoon."

"And what about my morale?"

"Amy... Don't you take him to visit Ofer and Etti in the afternoon?"

"They're not always there, Steve. But never mind, I'll be all right."

"Amy. Do you think it's easy here?"

"No, of course not. But why do we have to do things that are hard, Steve? Oh, I know, it's because it's in the sacred land. So everything's all right."

"Amy, I wish you wouldn't talk this way."

She said nothing. Behind me they were already making noise.

"I'll see about Thursday. I really can't promise. I'm sorry, they're pressuring me now."

"Bye."

She hung up.

"Damn, damn, damn."

Except for a few Israelis who'd left Israel before army age and come back, the Shalav Betniks in the platoon were immigrants from all over the world. North America, France, Ethiopia, and Argentina were the best represented. My circle of buddies mostly included "Anglo-Saxons" from English-speaking countries. But in the confusion of the first day, I'd wound up in a tent with seven Argentineans. They were nice guys, but they liked to do things in collective camaraderie—talk loudly together, agree loudly about things together, laugh loudly together. It may have had something with the fact that, back in Argentina, they'd all been in Habonim, a socialist-Zionist movement. In any case, as a more individualist type who treasured having time to himself, it kind of drove me crazy.

One of them, though, was Ricardo, and with him I got along. He had sandy hair, a bulbous nose, softly kind blue eyes. He was from a different walk of life entirely—an electrical engineer; but it didn't seem to matter. If I recall right, we first conversed one day when we happened to be the only ones in the tent around noon; we just hit it off. Now, when I got a guard duty with him, I always looked forward to it.

On this night we had to guard the *shin gimmel*, the gate of the base. During the day it was hard; there was a stream of vehicles entering the base, and the drivers of all the civilian ones had to be checked. And on top of that, you had to be on your toes; the area was mainly Palestinian, there was steady traffic on the road, and always the risk of an attack. I was surprised, actually, when after only about a week of training they started giving us *shin gimmel* duty—even during the day; but in those days the Israeli army had a "sink or swim," "you can do it because you've got no choice" ethos.

At night, though, it was easier. Only military vehicles came through; you just had to push a button that opened the gate and wave them on.

Ricardo and I, our M16 rifles cradled on our laps, sat on chairs behind the gate and at opposite sides of it, facing each other.

A warm September night. Across from us a silent ridge towered, with stars over it. It could have been one of the serenest places in the world.

We spoke Hebrew, which I've tried to render.

"Steven," Ricardo said. "You look...like someone who's heard very bad news."

I smiled. "I look that bad?"

I said, "It's my wife."

"Is everything OK?"

I said, "She doesn't want to be here."

"In Israel?"

"Right."

He said, "It's hard for her now."

"It is. But it always is. She always has the same complaint—why do we have to be here."

"Oh, Steven... Did she want to come here?"

"Not really. I talked her into it.... I thought she might like it once she's here."

"She doesn't like it?"

"She didn't find work in her field. She misses her family."

"My wife too. She misses the family. But both of us...were the same. I know her since Habonim—we were both in Habonim. We met there when we were thirteen. And for both of us it was clear—the future is Israel."

"You were lucky that way."

He said, "She asks to go back?"

"No. She doesn't ask to go back. But she makes my life difficult. She keeps letting me know she's unhappy."

"Oh, Steven... You look at the history—the Zionists were always a minority. Others came to Israel because they were refugees, they were desperate, they were persecuted. My grandparents came here from Poland in the 1920s. Not because they were Zionists. Because of the antisemites in Poland. The Zionists make the foundation, and others come—when they're desperate. The Jew who sees himself as safe and comfortable in the Diaspora—ninety-nine percent of the time, he does not want to come to Israel."

"Yes, Ricardo. It's true unfortunately."

"So you were the Zionist, and you tried to lead her here."

"And as of now I've failed."

We sat there quietly awhile. Suddenly the prayer calls from the surrounding villages—from loudspeakers in mosques—erupted; not quite synchronized, creating an eerie effect of cacophony.

"Steven," he said. "We make *aliyah* to Israel. This is Jordan."

"What?"

"This is Jordan, Steven. We have to get out of here. We have nothing to look for here."

"It stopped being Jordan after the Six Day War."

"I know. But it still is."

He paused—as if to give the muezzins their say.

"Ricardo, you walk to the top of any of these hills around here—and they're not very high hills—and you know what you see? You see Tel Aviv. This area, this high ground, controls the country. Eighty percent of the country is along the coast, Ricardo, from Tel Aviv up to Haifa. You give these hills to whoever's going to take them, it's called strategic suicide."

"Steven. We're not strong?"

"We're strong, Ricardo. Have you talked to people who were here for the Six Day War? We were strong then too. People walked around with white faces. They were digging mass graves. All the Jordanians had to do was cut through to the coast—nine miles, Ricardo—and it would have been the end of Israel. And they would have started right here. In these hills."

A jeep pulled up at the gate. I leaned over, pushed the button; the gate opened slowly, creakily. The jeep pulled up between us. The soldier on my side, the passenger side, held something out to me; it was a box of chocolate chips. I took a couple of them.

"Everything OK?" he said.

"Everything OK."

"Good! Good night to you guys!"

"Good night to you guys too."

They drove on into the base; I pushed the button and the gate creakily closed.

"Steven," Ricardo said. "These things that you're saying—you write them in your articles?"

"Yes, I do, actually."

"Oh, it's too bad. I hope you don't become prime minister."

"I don't think you need to worry."

"What if there's peace, Steven?"

"Ricardo, what's peace? An Arab leader signs a piece of paper. Even if he's sincere, can you make his country be peaceful for another five years, another ten years? Is this a peaceful area? They fight with each other more than they fight with us."

"We don't have peace with Egypt, Steven?"

"Official peace, Ricardo. The hatred for Israel is the same. The same as it was before the peace treaty. The leadership does nothing about it —if they do anything, they encourage it. But let's say the so-called peace with Egypt breaks down. They want to attack us again? They have to go through the Sinai. Two days, Ricardo—two days before they reach us. They attack us from here? They don't have to go through anything. They're already almost at the coast."

"Steven. Zionism means a Jewish state. It doesn't mean ruling over people who hate us."

"Ricardo, since '67 we've made their lives a lot better. Their health care, their life expectancy—way up. Number of homes with running water and electricity—way up, almost like us.

They hate us anyway? What can I do about it? It doesn't mean I give them land to attack us from."

"Yes, Steven, you can say, their living standards are higher, they have more of this and that. But people want to be free. Living under occupation is not what people want."

"Free, Ricardo? What freedom do people have in Arab countries? I know, people say, 'We cannot deny them political rights.' What political rights do people have in Arab countries? They might vote for parliaments that everyone knows are a joke. There's a dictator and his clique and that's who rules them."

"Steven, those are their own people ruling them. Occupation is something else. Someone else ruling them. It's humiliating to them. It's something different."

"Ricardo, we can't rush things. We have to let things evolve. The less they attack us the more we can give them self-rule. We can't give them self-rule while they're attacking us. We have to get that through to them. First they have to stop hating us and stop teaching their kids to hate us. If they do, we can give them autonomy, or federation with Jordan, or who knows what. I know, you'll say—that's backwards, the occupation causes the hate. First get rid of the occupation. Not really, Ricardo. The hate was there before the occupation, a long time before it. I think you know that. And some of this land we can't give up no matter what, because you can't defend Israel without it. Zionism means a Jewish state that you can defend."

"Steven, you are the militant Zionist. You are Jabotinsky. And I am the Zionist who will always look for peace."

"I'll always look for it too, Ricardo. But not where it can't be found."

"I know, that's what all of you say. Can't be found. Can't be found." He sighed.

The muezzins had stopped; we sat quietly. There was still a long way to go until midnight, when we were supposed to be relieved—but only if our replacements showed up in time; sometimes they ambled along five or ten minutes late. The theory was that we would have five hours to sleep, midnight to five. But even if the replacements came when they were supposed to, it took time to go back to the tents, unload the gear, lie down on the cot and fall asleep. And it would seem like no time at all before the drill sergeant's voice split the dawn air with *"Kulam hahutza!"*—everyone out.

February 7-8, 1995

10

A February morning in the German Colony, 1995. The German Colony—named so because, starting in the nineteenth century, members of a German religious society lived there—is a delightful neighborhood in southern Jerusalem. Its main street, Emek Refaim, is lined with cafes and boutiques. In its side streets you see old buildings from the Ottoman and British Mandate periods.

I was sitting on the outdoor patio of a café on the corner of Emek Refaim and Wingate Street. I was working on an article, drinking hot coffee in the cold, scintillant winter air. ("Winter"—not at all like where I grew up, snow being a rarity, but still a distinct season.) About three years earlier we'd bought a two-story apartment on Wingate Street and moved there from Maale Adumim. Maale Adumim was then still a young, developing community, and our apartment there was already worth a lot more than when we'd bought it; we realized that we could, just barely, achieve a move into Jerusalem by selling it. Also, in 1989, Galia (named after my father's mother) had been born, and the Maale Adumim place was very small for the four of us.

Meanwhile the world had advanced technologically; laptop computers were already a common sight in cafes. Being, though, tech-shy and slow to adapt, I still preferred to write a first draft with pen and paper—if time allowed—then take it home to type on the desktop computer in the very small room I called my study.

I sat back from the writing, gazed at the stone building across the street with its pleasing latticework and winter flowers in pots. Lital, in her beige waitress dress, stepped out of the indoor part of the café. Her eyes fixed on me, she walked over to my table.

She said, "*Efshar la'azor l'cha, adon?*"—can I help you, sir?

I answered, also in Hebrew, "Yes, I'd like French toast and a beer."

"Beer in the morning, sir?"

"Yes, please."

"Fine. I think it's just the thing to go with your French toast."

"Lital," I said, "I'm writing now. Really."

"Why are you so mean to me, sir?"

"I'm not mean to you."

"Yes you are."

"No I'm not."

"Yes you are."

I gazed up at her. Lital was one of those occasional Israelis with blond hair; it was long, straight, and lustrous. She had grey eyes with long lashes. Her body—I sometimes called her Litali, which is what "lethal" would sound like in Hebrew—was lithe and sloped in the beige dress.

She said, "I miss you."

"You don't have to miss me, I'm here almost every day."

"You know what I mean."

"Lital. We're not there anymore."

"Why not?"

"You know why."

"No, I don't. Explain it to me."

"Because I'm back with my wife."

"But you were with her then."

"I know. But I wasn't with her."

"She knew about it then?"

"Only at the end."

"So now she doesn't have to know about it."

"Lital, I can't do that."

"Why?"

"Because I'm really trying to be married now."

"That didn't matter before?"

"It mattered. But the situation with my wife was different."

"So now you're the big family man."

"Lital, I can see your boss in there. He's probably looking at you and thinking, what's she doing hanging around talking to that guy, instead of working."

"Yeah, Steve, you're right."

She started to move away; turned and said, "You're cruel to me."

"Lital, you're right. I'm trouble. I screw up everywhere I go."

Amy and I had fallen on hard times. It was a long, gradual process; but over the past year or so we'd hit bottom, or near it. Our intimate life had dwindled until there wasn't much left of it; at night I often slept on the cot in my study. We told the kids: "Abba works late and doesn't want to wake Ema up when he comes in the room." There was some truth to it, even if things had been all right between us; I did tend to work late and Amy was a light sleeper.

She told me—these were calm conversations, without shouting—that she'd subordinated her life to mine for too long and could no longer put aside the resentment she felt; it made her "turn cold to me." She said she blamed herself. From the beginning—in those days almost twenty years ago after my father died, when I'd come home on weekends to be with my mother, and would get together with Amy—I'd talked about *aliyah*. She said she'd assumed it wasn't serious, that after some sort of life took shape for me in America I'd forget about it. And when I kept talking about it, and she saw that I was serious, she let herself get swept along by it—and by everything I did. She said she could have asserted herself, and should have. Now, though, it had become too much for her.

After a few years of being impressed with her work, of observing her knack for organizing and running things, the bookstore chain had offered her a post as manager of a new, small branch in a different part of Jerusalem, and she'd accepted it. But, though the pay was pretty good—it was one of the reasons we could move to the Colony—the work just wasn't that interesting or fulfilling to her. I told her it wouldn't hurt, meanwhile, to make a couple of inquiries about social work; she did, but they were rebuffed. I encouraged her to keep trying. She said there weren't openings for someone in her late thirties; it wasn't worth it. I still thought she should keep trying, but she didn't agree.

It didn't help, in terms of how she felt, that for me *aliyah* had been a boon. I'd kept publishing articles in the *Jerusalem Post*, in American Jewish magazines, and now sometimes I was getting a piece into bigger, mass-market American outlets too. It was very fulfilling to me; I was helping Israel, getting ego boosts, and getting paid. And along with the freelance editing in English, I'd taken up translating from Hebrew to English.

So I ran a sort of three-ring freelance circus, and it did well—though, of course, earnings for such activities are far from dramatic. For the editing and translating my clientele had gone beyond Hebrew University to some of the other universities and think tanks; more and more people sought me out. So the overall feeling was good, and *aliyah* had made it all possible.

Not that it was all good, of course. I still harbored the sense that fiction was my true calling, but apart from writing a short story now and then I had no time and energy to devote to it. Sending the short stories to literary journals wasn't like sending out the political articles; they came back with brusque rejections. As for the novel I'd started to write long ago in Renford Park, it remained in storage; I never even took it out to look at it. I'd hardly forgotten it; it was still on my mind—"it." I knew that, precarious as things were with Amy, starting with "that" again could sink the boat.

Then, in the previous spring, something else had happened: Amy's mother's cancer had worsened. She needed a couple of operations, and the basic outlook—she knew—wasn't good. Amy's father was a decent man but impatient, or inept, with emotion, not much for giving support. Her brother had turned out to be a kind of drifter; he was meanwhile in St. Louis bouncing among various jobs. Her sister was a solid person, but she lived in Los Angeles and she, too, couldn't be in Renford Park much. For Amy the situation was the worst possible materialization of her fears and misgivings about *aliyah*; it weighed on her very heavily that she could barely be with her mother. She flew there a couple of times for visits, taking the kids with her; but it was hard for her to get away from work and the visits were short.

For Amy it all came together and she—it was our euphemism for it—"turned cold to me." That side of things had been declining already for years, but now it almost stopped. Then in about August, Lital joined the staff at the café. Her flirting was constant, tinged with something desperate. Finally, one day, standing by my table, she asked me what I was working on. I explained that I was a writer. Usually it doesn't exactly lower your stock with women. In turn, I found out that she was a fourth-year accounting student at Hebrew University (she was twenty-five, having started there after her two years of army service and one year of post-army travel). I started thinking about her a lot. It was an infatuation, but a strong one—especially when Amy was precluding anything else from happening. In September, Lital was still alone in the Jerusalem flat she rented with two roommates; they were from out of town, and the semester only started in October. So one afternoon—under constant flirting—I gave in and went with her to her apartment.

Once it started, naturally, it kept going. After some visits to Lital, I decided to tell Amy about it. It had happened to me once before; it seemed I was just wasn't cut out to harbor a lie all the time. After initially throwing a cup across the living room, she calmed down; she said—OK, that's it, let's put an end to it. I told her I was sorry it had happened, would not have wanted it, and suggested we go to a marriage counselor. After a couple more days, I was surprised when she said she was willing to give it a try.

The counselor, Ariela, asked Amy if she would accept a quid pro quo where I would stop going to Lital and we, Amy and I, would try to get back on track. Amy—not easily—agreed. Ariela put emphasis on Amy's awareness that she, herself, had chosen to make *aliyah* with me; that I—though I'd pressured her—had not forced her, something no one could have done. She also evoked the positive feelings that Amy still had toward me. She pointed out that those feelings had something to do with my idealistic bent, which, in turn, had something to do with my yen to move to Israel.

Though, again, for Amy in particular it wasn't easy, we tried recharging the marriage. Sometimes we seemed to recapture old moments, old gleams; sometimes there was an air of gloom, of resignation about her. The situation with her mother very seriously got her down, and she couldn't seem to stop associating the problem with me. We kept going to Ariela, and, of course, "the kids" were another major theme—that it was probably better for them if we could stick it out. Meanwhile, at the café, I had Lital on my hands. I considered switching to another café, and should have; I was just too addicted to how perfect it was there for writing—the patio in the morning, the bright blooms across the street. Lital gave me sidelong, condemnatory looks; I was saved by the protocol against consorting with customers. Sometimes, though, she managed to sneak in little verbal exchanges with me, and it was never too pleasant.

After this latest tiff with Lital I found that I couldn't keep writing. Over the years I'd become proficient at walling out various kinds of "noise"—from music in cafes to problems of life—while writing. This spat with Lital, though, had been bitterer than previous ones. I looked at the page with my scrawled writing, but I couldn't focus on it. The article wasn't really urgent, but I'd budgeted this morning for finishing the written draft and taking it home and typing it. That was gone now.

When I got home the place had the pleasant midday quiet it had when no one else was there—Amy at work, the kids at school. It took up the second and third stories of one side of the building. The second story, our lower floor, had the living room, kitchen, and the kids' bedrooms; the upper floor had the parents' bedroom, the study, and a room we called "the TV room" where there was a TV in addition to the one in the living room.

I went upstairs to the bedroom. I tossed my knapsack and coat on the bed, pried off my shoes. I went to the "study"—really an alcove, looking out on Wingate Street. The computer was still on from earlier in the morning. Without sitting down, I moved the mouse so as to enter my Speedmail.

In the column of six newly arrived emails, the fifth from the top caught my eye:

ConnieLn

I gazed at it.

I sat slowly down in the chair.

I opened it.

Steve!!

How are you!?!? I wouldn't be surprised if this is kind of amazing to you. But amazing things happen in this world.

The other day I was leafing through a copy of *USA Today* at work. On the opinion page I came upon an article about Israel by one Steve Sandorsky!

You'll forgive me if, before reading the article, I let my eyes travel down to the bio note at the end of it.

I read—I've got it memorized!—"Steve Sandorsky is a writer and translator in Jerusalem. Reach him at S-Sandor@speedmail.co.il."

Oh my God, that must be him!!!

Actually, S-Sandor, I knew it was you. Still in touch with a few people from school, I heard years ago that you married Amy Goldberg and moved to Israel with her! It sounds wonderful and I hope it's all going well for you and Amy!

I would love to hear more, Steve, about your life there—from what I know about the Holy Land, it's a very intense place!

As for me, I'm writing to you from Waukee, Iowa, which is a suburb of Des Moines. I work in Des Moines for the state Parks and Recreation Department. How much you might know about my story for these last twenty years or so, I don't know. If you're curious I would be glad to fill you in. It's not always the most cheerful story, but it probably doesn't surprise you at all to know that!

So, Steve—if you have a free moment from your busy life of writing and translating in Jerusalem—I'd love to hear from you!

Your dear friend always,

Connie

PS—Great article by the way!!

I sat there without moving.
I sank my face into both hands.
I said, "Connie..."

11

I knew I'd answer, but for the time being I couldn't. I went to the bedroom, lay down on my back on the bed.

I said again—this time in more of a whisper—"Connie…"

Lying that way, I fell asleep; I hadn't slept much the night before, or been sleeping well in general lately.

A few hours later I was woken up by sounds of Amy down below in the kitchen. Or maybe I'd been waking up anyway, and then heard them.

Amy, as boss of the store, had somewhat flexible hours, and sometimes came home fairly early in the afternoon. I looked—it was about three o'clock.

I knew I'd go down there; but first I lay still for another minute.

It was dawning on me that, now that she'd made contact with me again, there was no reason I'd ever lose contact with her again. She was back—for good. It did not seem possible.

I saw high leaves waving in a summer breeze in Renford Park.

I wouldn't say that the years had been kind to Amy, or that they'd been unkind to her—it was a mixed result. She'd put on weight—not too much, but a pit portly. The soft, girlish sparkle wasn't much in her eyes anymore; though sometimes it returned when she saw Lior, or Galia, or both. Her eyes—especially in this latest period—were a duller black; but together with the lines around her mouth, her still-long, flowing hair, I saw a kind of careworn beauty. I'd still have found her fetching if I was first meeting her, though in a different key.

When I came into the kitchen she was standing by the counter where a coffeepot was lit and starting to make noises. I went over, gingerly took her arm and kissed her cheek.

"Just get up?" she said.

"Yeah. Tired…"

"Coffee?"

"Yeah, sure."

I went to the table, slumped into a chair; I rubbed my eyes and sighed.

She brought me a coffee, but went back to the counter and stood leaning into it, holding her cup.

"So," I said. "How was work?"

"Oh, God…"

She said, "An insane French tourist came in who kept asking for a book, but no one could understand him. Finally there was an Israeli from France who understood him and translated for him—*The Morrison Guide to Birds of the Holy Land.*"

"Did you have it?"

"Yeah."

"In English?"

"Yeah."

"Wait—he couldn't say the title in English but he had to have the book in English?"

"Yup."

"That doesn't make sense."

"I know."

"Ha-ha."

We both sipped our coffee.

She said, "How about you?"

"Oh…the usual. Wrote a little in the morning, did some translating, just now I was taking a nap."

She said, "Steve, how do you feel about things?"

I said, "About what?"

"What we're doing. You and me."

I considered. "I'm glad we're trying again. I know it's not easy…especially for you. I feel good about it."

She held her cup, pondered; a line beside her mouth deepened.

She said, "I don't know. I feel…maybe it's too much for me."

She said, "I don't know."

I said, "I thought we were trying."

"We're trying. I don't know. It's…I feel like I don't have energy. I don't have strength."

My cup was now on the table; I stared somberly at it.

She said, "I want to take the kids again to visit my parents, for Passover. You can come too, if you can get away from work. I think I can get away from the store for ten days or something like that. Once I'm there, though…I don't know."

The door to the house opened; we heard the rapid, light footsteps of Galia. She ran into the kitchen, her satchel flying behind her. Amy said "*Ga-liii*!!" with a look of desperate joy. Gali said "*E-maaa*!!" and jumped into her arms.

"We made a picture for Tu Bishvat!" Gali said (in English; we mostly spoke English with the kids). Tu Bishvat, which was the next day, is a kind of Jewish Arbor Day that falls in late January or early February. In Israel at that time you can see the first white and pink almond blossoms. Lior's class was on a tree-planting field trip to the Galilee.

Gali—with blond hair from my mother's side and dark eyes from the Jewish side, now intensely lit—yanked her picture from her satchel and held it before Amy.

"*Nice!*" Amy said. "Show it to Abba!"

"Abba, look!!" Gali said, dashing to me, holding the picture close to my face. It showed an almond tree with large, discrete purple leaves, a light blue sky and a white cloud in the background.

"*Nice!*" I said. "Beautiful, Gali!" I grabbed her and kissed her.

"Ema, I'm going to the TV room!" she said. "There's a Tu Bishvat special!"

"Don't you want a snack, sweetheart?" said Amy.

"Can you *bring* the snack to the TV room?"

"OK, sweetheart, I'll bring it."

She dashed out.

I said, in the stillness, "Amy, what were you saying before?"

"Before?"

"About taking the kids to your parents' house, and staying there."

"What?"

"That's what you said, isn't it?"

"No, it's not. I said it would be hard for me to come back. That's a little different, isn't it?"

"And what happens if we split up?"

The words landed like a large stone in a lake.

139

"What happens? I don't know. You tell me, Steve. What do you think happens?"

"I don't know. You tell me. I think maybe you'll want to realize your long-lost dream of getting out of this place."

She took a big sigh, rubbing her face in her hand.

"Steve, I wouldn't do that to you, OK? I wouldn't do it to the kids either. I wouldn't want them to grow up far away from you."

I sat silent.

I said, "So it's not so much Israel you want to get free of. It's me."

She sighed again.

"OK. I'm sorry I brought this up. We've got Ariela in a couple of days, don't we?"

"Yeah. On Thursday."

"OK. Want to wait till then to go into these things?"

"Sure."

We both fell silent. We could hear the faint din of the TV.

She said, "I need to bring Gali something."

I said, "I better go up and do some work."

When I looked out the window of the study, all the way down the street—to the right, the opposite direction from the café and Emek Refaim—I could see an almond tree, its white blossoms bright in the waning sun.

A couple more work-related emails had arrived. I answered them, and also the ones from the morning I hadn't answered yet.

I opened Connie's email again.

I gazed at it in what was still disbelief.

I reread it.

I loved most "but it probably doesn't surprise you at all to know that!"—because it alluded to, acknowledged, our past awareness of each other—and "Your dear friend always...."

So now I was going to answer her. I was going to write to her. To Connie.

First I lay back on the cot.

What time was it now in Iowa? Moving toward four in Jerusalem; so toward eight, eight in the morning, in Iowa. Morning; she'd probably be checking her emails....

I saw a high cloud through the window, catching a ray from the descending sun. I heard the din from the TV.

Dear Connie,

How inexpressibly wonderful to hear from you. The possibility had never crossed my mind. I'm always on a tech-lag; the thought never occurred to me that, in this brave new cyber world, such a thing is actually possible.

Yes, Connie, you heard right. Amy and I got married—going on 16 years ago; we moved to Israel—going on 11 years ago. We have two kids—Lior (12) and Galia (6). Lior, by the way, is a boy's name; I think that to non-Israeli ears it's probably clear that Galia is a girl's name, but I've been here long enough that I'm not even sure about that. They're named, by the way, after Louis and Greta, if you recall who they were after so many years.

Connie, what I've heard about your life is "Connie Landry moved to Iowa"—it was years ago,

and that was all. I think I'm even less in touch with
the old class of '72 than you seem to be. Please
fill me in!!—I could not be more curious. It does
sound like you have a nice job—working for the
Parks Department; it seems fitting for someone I
associate with the pastoral. That is, I hope it's nice,
but you can tell me.

My life in Jerusalem…I write my own works
in English, edit other people's works if they're in
English, and translate other people's works from
Hebrew to English, and as a freelancer inputting
diligently away here in my alcove overlooking Wingate Street, I do OK. Amy's also doing quite well—
manager of a branch of Steimatzky's bookstores in
Jerusalem. We live in a delightful southern-Jeru-
salem neighborhood known as the German Colony
(named after German Protestants who made a
colony out of it a century and a half ago). And you
may be surprised to learn also that I'm a soldier—a
member of a reserve unit, dropping everything to
do reserve duty when the call comes.

Connie,

I sat back; I had to wait out some emotion.
I resumed:

if this all sounds too rosy to be true, actually it
is. Our marriage hasn't been doing that well lately,
and despite efforts to improve it, I'm not sure it's
improving. If you're curious I'd be perfectly willing
to tell you more about this, but I don't want to
overwhelm you with too much in one email.

Lastly, Connie, along with the amazement and joy at getting your email, there's another impact…but I'm less certain about it. When we parted a long time ago, I guess you could say we weren't on good terms. That you're writing to me now, in a warm and friendly vein—seems to signal something to me…am I forgiven?

Connie, I know that people are busy and I've posed quite a few issues and questions to you in this mail—please do not feel pressured! Get to it when you can.

With great gratitude for approaching me again,

Steve

I sat back. I looked at it. I didn't have the strength to reread it. I clicked on "Send."

I got up and went to the window again.

Wingate Street was now in a stillness before dusk. The sky, formerly brilliant blue, was a duller blue, tinged with grey. Craning my neck, I could still make out the almond tree—dim white, soon to dissolve.

Orde Wingate was a British army officer who came to serve in prestate Israel in 1936. A devout Protestant, deeply rooted in the Bible, he viewed the Jews' return to the Land of Israel as a divine necessity, and he gave crucial guidance to the Haganah—the main Jewish militia at the time—in defending Jewish areas, even accompanying them in dangerous missions himself. By 1939 the British—by then staunchly pro-Arab and anti-Jewish—transferred him elsewhere, and he died in a plane crash in Burma in 1944.

I stood looking at Wingate Street.

I sighed deeply, went back to my chair and gazed at the screen. I hadn't gotten any work done today. There were three translation jobs waiting for me. Which one should I start on? I decided to have a look at each of them so I could choose which one, and began clicking.

I stopped.

Connie could—possibly—have received my email and be reading it now....

My cell phone, which was in my pocket, erupted. In those days you picked a tune to be your cell phone's ring. I'd picked "Waltzing Matilda," which I've always found one of the most poignant melodies in the world. But it leapt from my cell phone with a sort of cutting fury that always befuddled me and jangled my nerves. I yanked the phone from my pocket and desperately pushed icons so the noise would stop.

"*Ken*," I said.

"*Lama ata hoshev sh'mutar l'cha lesahek im anishim?*"

It was Lital: Why do you think it's OK for you to play with people?

"Lital. I did not play with you."

"Yes. You did."

"Lital. It was something we both chose. If there was someone who got it started it was you. You know that."

"Steve, why do you lie? You exploited it. You got what you wanted out of It, and then you threw me away."

"Lital, you know that's not true. You know that the situation with me and my wife changed."

"Steve, you think I buy that? You think I'm that naïve?"

"Lital, it doesn't matter if you're naïve or not. It's the truth."

"The truth is that you used me to get what you wanted and then you threw me away."

"Lital, that is not—"

She cut the connection.

I set the phone down by the computer.

I sat back. I put my face in my hands. "Jesus Christ."

Amy, Gali, and I had our Tu Bishvat dinner. It was Tu Bishvat now; the Jewish day starts at sunset. Amy and I didn't look at each other much. For dessert Amy served traditional Tu Bishvat foods—dates, figs, almonds, dried apricots, dried pineapple. Gali rendered a judgment that dried pineapple was her favorite food.

Back upstairs in the study, now dark outside, I at last got to work, picking one of the translating jobs. Of course, I checked my emails. One work-related one, some spam. Nothing from Connie yet.

After a little while, though, an email arrived—from NellS at bostonu.edu.

Unlike me, so far Nellie Sandorsky-Cohen seemed able to sail through life without serious problems. With her PhD in Romance languages from Yale, she was now a professor of French and Italian at Boston University. There she'd met Joel Cohen, a young professor of European history. They had two girls, Rachel and Debbie. Oddly—since Joel was Jewish—from a genetic standpoint Rachel and Debbie were, like my kids, three-quarters Jewish; yet, unlike mine, they didn't count as Jewish, since Nellie didn't.

For Thanksgiving and the Fourth of July, and sometimes Chanukah-Christmas, Nellie, Joel, and the kids would go to Schenectady to join my mother and Ed, and one or more of

Ed's sons if they were in town, for the holiday. I was welded to Israel, but it always made me sad when it happened.

Nellie wrote:

Hi Steve, how's it going? Joel and I read your *Jerusalem Post* piece online. My my, what a sizzler! Burns out the screen as you're reading it! But it left both of us, I must confess, hoping that you're wrong. I dunno—a glimmer of hope? A spark of optimism? Anywhere?

Cheers,

Nellie

I smiled. I shook my head.

S-Sandor: Nellie, I would gladly embrace some optimism if there were the slightest warrant for it, if this whole Oslo scam, this faux peace process, was anything but an utter fraud and a hoax. Those quotes I gave from Arafat—they're real, I didn't make them up. If peace is befalling us, why is he still talking—in Arabic, of course—about jihad and the Treaty of Hudaybiyyah? Now that he's been set up in the West Bank with land, guns, loads of aid money, and power, terror attacks are sharply on the upswing. You think there's no connection? Wish I could put an optimistic spin on it, Little Nell. I'm just reacting to what's going on out there in the real world, and for that I'll get pilloried as a naysayer if not a warmonger.

As for how I'm doing…I wish there, too, the tidings were rosy. Based on my assessment of reality, though, I'd say my marriage is in trouble. Nellie, I know things are a little complex here, that my wife is your best friend from early childhood and that you and she are in touch a lot. I don't want to put you in an uncomfortable, impossible position. So if you ask how I'm doing, that has to be part of the answer, but it's totally understandable to me that you might want to leave it at that.

Other stuff is happening to me too, but I think that sufficient unto the day—or more than sufficient—is what I've already written.

Steve

I sent it; went back into the file with the translation. I stared at the crowd of Hebrew and English words. I had to concentrate now. Had to. Had to wall it all out and get to work.

I did; but after not much time there was a ding.

It was a reply from Nellie:

Little Nell!! I thought you weren't much of a Dickens man!!

Yes, Steve, regarding what you mentioned, I've been kept more or less updated on it. And as for me being in an uncomfortable position…what can I say. You're my brother; Amy is my best friend from the dim mists of childhood. Who has the better claim? I really can't say, but I can say that there's no reason you shouldn't tell me whatever you might feel like telling me. Of course, anything either of you would tell me in confidence would be kept that way; but if I communicate with both of you about this, then that won't be kept a secret from either of you.

Steve, to begin with you should know that I'm your advocate. I've been distressed by what's happening and am still hoping things will work out. I do understand, from listening to Amy, that attitudes have built up in her over the years that she can't just nullify. But I think the argument for doing the utmost to get over that…well, it's a strong argument (fit for a *Jerusalem Post* polemic!?). It has to do with you being a worthy person, and of course, with the situation of a family with young kids.

I was aware of the effort being made lately to get over the problem, and I was feeling more optimistic. You seem to be saying things aren't actually going so well?

Well, Steve, feel free to say whatever you wish—or if you wish, because the situation is too tricky, to leave it at that—understood!

S-Sandor: No, not much of a Dickens man. The novels by him I read in college—and I sort of liked at least *Our Mutual Friend*—seem to have gone in one ear and out the other. Don't seem to connect with the guy.

Yes, Nellie, I too thought things were—slowly—getting better; we've been going to the counselor, you presumably know, and I thought it was helping. Today, though, Amy sounded negative again. She said she didn't have the strength to keep going with it. She said she wants to take the kids to her parents' house for Passover and that I could come, too, but she knows it's hard for me to get away from my work (calling it an "invitation" would be an exaggeration). Then she seemed to say that once she was there she (and the kids) might not even come back. When I pressed her on that, she denied that was what she meant; she just said she meant it would be very hard to come back—that is, to me. Anyway, the message wasn't encouraging.

NellS: Steve, I'm very sorry to hear this. If she's even fantasizing about "escaping" then things may not be improving as we wish. Oy!

I know that the situation with her mother is getting her down. There's something else that has occurred to me, it's just a thought, a hunch, a guess, and there might not be anything to it. Do you think Amy might feel better if—at some point—you'd converted? I have the feeling that there's something in the background that weighs on her, something she doesn't like to talk about. I want to stress that she has *never* implied to me in any way that your converting or not converting is an issue for her. So, this may be wild, baseless speculation....

S-Sandor: Nellie, it's funny you should mention that about converting, since—you might recall—it was from Amy that I found out indirectly, when I was 11, that I wasn't Jewish, after years of assuming I was. Have I continued to fail the test?

I dunno; Amy has always claimed to me that it doesn't matter to her, that she considers me Jewish. On the other hand...does she see me as a non-Jew who bosses Jews around, tells them where they have to live? Something keeps getting her down, that's for sure. Did you hear about my peccadillo?

I used to think off and on about converting, but I stopped because I realized it was just abstract thinking, not something I was really inclined to do. You know how we grew up—so distant from any form of religion. In the end, I guess I couldn't give rabbis such authority over me—to set out a course I'd have to follow to "become," to be recognized as, a Jew. So I settled for being what I appear fated to be—a non-Jewish Zionist. There are some good precedents, like the guy they named my street after.

NellS: Oh yes, I recall when you found out you weren't Jewish! It was in one of our late-night palavers! I recall that for days after that you looked stricken. At the time I didn't understand it. I think I do now.

Though I'd say "non-Jewish Zionist" is a bit too blunt—there's Jewishness in us! These things are about as complex as they can be.

And yes, I heard about your peccadillo. Oy, not a good move. I know it happened at a time when the marriage was on hold. Amy realizes that too. But…while hardly a hidebound conservative, I fear there's always a risk in that kind of thing.

And apart from all that, I so hope you and she can get back on the right track again!

S-Sandor: I hope for it too, Nellie, but I wouldn't put a lot of money on it right now. We've got another session with the counselor in a couple of days, so we'll have to see how it goes. There's other stuff happening with me too, but instead of going into it I should probably get back to this translation work, which I've been dodging almost all day.

NellS: Yes, and I have a class to teach in less than an hour! I fear I may have to be at my improvisatory best! Feel free to update me whenever you wish—including about "other stuff"!

S-Sandor: OK, Nell, I'll sign off for now. Till next.

NellS: Bye.

Around ten o'clock I went into our bedroom. Amy was on her side of the bed, wearing a track suit, her glasses on, reading a book that was propped on the fronts of her thighs, a lit lamp and a small electric heater on the night table beside her.

I lay down on my back next to her, one hand behind my head, looking up at the ceiling.

I said, "Lior call?"

"No. They're back tomorrow afternoon."

I said, "If I'd converted—would that have made you feel better about things?"

She closed the book, leaving it propped; she took off the glasses, put them on the night table, and turned to look at me.

"What makes you ask that now?"

"I don't know. Nothing special. Just thinking about all kinds of things while I'm working."

She said, "If you'd converted, would that have made me feel better...."

She said, "Haven't I told you that it doesn't matter to me?"

"Yes, that is what you've told me. But..."

"But?"

"I don't know. I just thought...maybe anyway."

She said, "If you felt like converting—if that's what you want to do—it would be fine—I would have no objection to it."

"Which...isn't that much of an answer."

She said, "Steve, I'm not the tribunal. You live here, you serve in the army, your father was Jewish."

I said, "I didn't get much work done today. I'm going to have to keep going for a while."

"OK."

When I was at the door, she said, "Who were you talking to before?"

I turned.

"What?"

"After supper. You were in your study. You raised your voice a couple of times."

"It was Lital."

"Lital..."

"Yeah, she's still on my case. Accusing me of things."

"Still?"

"Yeah, still. What can I do."

"And you're still going there every day, right?"

"What, the café? Amy, I've told you, it's the best place for writing."

I said, "OK, I'll stop going there. I'll go to Caffit instead. I'm sure it'll be fine."

She said, "Aa, what difference does it make."

I stared at her.

She said, "With you there's always something going on."

I said, "What the hell is that supposed to mean?"

"With you there's always something going on."

I said, "You're still talking about *that*? Something when I was a kid?"

"Whatever."

I stood there for another moment; went out and closed the door.

In the study I stood in the almost-dark, only the computer screen lighting the room.

No. All the time since she'd been home, I'd been with her—talking or eating—or in the study. There was no point at which she could have come into the study and peeked at anything. It wasn't the sort of thing she did anyway.

I gave a peek myself. Still no email from Connie.

12

ConnieLn: Steve, thank you so much for your lovely reply! It showed up in my computer at work in the morning—in truth, it wasn't easy for me to concentrate on my work for the rest of the day! But now I'm home, and the house is quiet (definitely not an unmixed blessing—my son Benny is out with the gang as usual). For you it's—by my calculation—the middle of the night, so this email will—I hope—be a nice surprise for you when you check your mail in the morning.

To start with, I'm truly sorry your marriage has run into trouble. Of course you should feel free to tell me about it! It sounds so beautiful—a family in Israel with two young kids; I would always "root" for such a team to succeed! Did you have to convert to Judaism in order to move there? And Steve—of course I remember who Louis and Greta were! How could I ever forget their picture there in that room—so silent, the looks on their faces.... So beautiful that you named your kids after them, and that it worked out just right—a boy followed by a girl. Steve, in all candor, you should know that I'm writing this email with a tissue box handy. And it is actually not the first time today that I've had to resort to a tissue box—I had to be kind of clandestine about it at work!

What are the strains in your marriage? Have you tried a marriage counselor? Does it have to do with pressures of being immigrants? And a soldier too!—out of the whole Renford High class of '72, I have no doubt your biography is unique. But please explain this to me—how much of the year do you have to spend soldiering? Does that add to the strains? (I would think so, if it's a lot!) And please keep yourself safe! Is it dangerous? (I'm not sure I want to know, but you're permitted—you're *required*—to answer.) I know that, whether people are soldiers or not, there are dangers in Israel. I keep up with what's happening there. I know that you're there, after all. But sometimes I hear and read about things that are so terribly upsetting and I get very very anxious....

Steve, there is so much to catch up on—let's take it slow, OK? If I say everything I have to say, and answer all the questions in your email the way they deserve, this will be one of the world's longest emails. So for now just a few more things.

One big thing—how are Nellie and your mother??

My work at the Parks Department—yes it's on the whole quite nice, and I'm not displeased that I seem to be something of an earth goddess in your memory, "associated with the pastoral"! I'm almost embarrassed to say—to you—that the work mostly involves writing! I write loads of brochures and fliers about the parks and natural attractions of the state of Iowa, and I also do some PR work—taking visiting dignitaries and the like for tours of our parks, going to meetings to plan PR strategies, etc. etc. Mostly I sit there grinding out brochures; kind of strange, isn't it, that my work is somewhat like—well, a little—yours, even though you have a much bigger readership!

Steve, 22 years is so much to catch up on, and I really want—I'm aching—to fill in this huge blank for you. And I will. For now, though, with this email already not short, I'll give the most concise summary possible: I've been divorced for 15 years and my son Benny is 15. More later. And as you may have noticed, my last name is the same—I changed it back after the divorce.

And as for your big question...

Sorry—tissue break...

Steve, you were always forgiven. From the very moment— well, very soon after—when you told me what had happened. Because I have a rational side that sees things clearly—it's the less rational side that gets me in trouble. I understood how sorry you were, how honest you were (you didn't have to tell me but wanted to clear things up between us), how sweet, that you were stoned when it happened....

I'm going to have to go out and buy cartons of tissue boxes....

OK. You were always forgiven because I knew the truth. Knew that my reaction was way too extreme. But I *could not control it*. What happened touched all my fears and I *could not control it*....

Steve, I was *so cruel to you*....

Your friend forever,

Connie

S-Sandor: Yes, Connie, this is a tearful reunion....

I'm here. Burning the midnight oil, the post-midnight oil, in my study. I haven't been sleeping much at night lately, with all the pressures—mainly from the marriage—weighing me down. I've been catching naps during the day and exploiting the nighttime hours to get work done and other things...like, at present, placating myself with a fine cabernet sauvignon from the Golan Heights....

Connie, before anything else—you really shouldn't come down on yourself so harshly. Nobody is exactly crazy about finding out that their lover betrayed them. Reactions tend to be extreme. Yes, it was rough on me. But on you too.

On the brighter side, Nellie and my mother are doing great. Nellie is a prof of Romance languages at Boston University, married, with two girls. My mother remarried a few years after my father died, and she and her second husband are living in Schenectady and now enjoying quite a pleasant retirement together.

And what's up with your mom?—and—I'm almost afraid to ask—your dad?

My marriage…let's see. It's Amy who's the dissident. Yes, we're going to counseling—for a while I thought it was helping, now I'm not so sure. She says resentments at me have built up over the years, and she can't put them aside anymore. I was the one who wanted to move to Israel, not Amy. I kept insisting, and you could say I pressured her into it though of course I didn't force her. (I didn't have to convert to Judaism to move here, and I haven't.) She was afraid of not finding work in her field here—social work—and very perturbed about going to live so far from her family in the States. And now she could say that her darkest fears have materialized. She manages a small branch of a bookstore chain, but it's just a job to her, not what—she thinks—she really wanted. And now her mother is quite ill, and Amy can't be with her much, and this is really eating away at her, all the time. She says she made her life secondary to mine, and now she thinks it was all a mistake. She sees me as having done well here—which is true, actually—and herself as just having tagged along and now leading a bleak life (as she sees it).

Does this mean we're heading for the big D? She's hinting that we might be, but I still can't say for sure (he wrote, pouring himself another glass).

Soldiering. In '87—three years after we moved here—I did four months of training. Two months of basic training (hell on wheels), two months of learning how to shoot artillery guns so I could be in the artillery corps. Since then, reserve duty has usually been two stints a year—a longer one (about a month) and a shorter one (two to three weeks). We do stuff that has nothing at all to do with artillery and I haven't touched an artillery gun once since training so diligently on them (at the Israeli taxpayer's expense, of course). We mostly patrol Arab villages in the West Bank, in jeeps or on foot, and they're not the real flashpoints because we're an ordinary unit, not an elite unit, so they don't send us to the real flashpoints. So you shouldn't worry. I can't say that there's no danger at all but there's not that much. Same is true of Israel in general. For every bad incident you see on TV, there are ten thousand "incidents" that are just normal life. Danger's everywhere, after all, unfortunately.

Yes, the reserve duty does add strains to the marriage. Sometimes Amy pressures me to cook up some story and get out of it, but I've never done it.

Connie, your work sounds really nice. What degree did you get at Oneonta? If you even continued there—even that I don't know.

Connie, I still can't believe this is happening....

Connie...

Yes, the breakup was sheer hell for me. Sheer hell. Which is not to say I wasn't responsible for it—I was, at least as much as you, more than you. I went right away to a shrink and I was lucky because it was a great one, Bob Sivers. I was in very deep depression but he urged me to try to get through it without meds, and in those days I went to him twice a week and even called him sometimes, and I got through. He had a great insight—that I was inwardly aching to learn more about the Jewish side of the things, but inhibited from doing so because I wasn't actually a Jew. So as a constructive (and also—to the extent it was possible—distracting) activity, I launched my own course of Jewish studies—just very intensive reading, whatever I could get my hands on, the history and literature and everything. I did this on top of my course work at Winslow, but it wasn't that hard because I turned into a loner and had almost no social life, so I had time. I felt—rightly, I guess—that the other kids there couldn't possibly know or understand what was going on inside me, the pain and the grappling with the pain, and that there was a wall between me and them. And that was pretty much how it was for about three years until the next big milestone—my father's death, and the thing starting with Amy—the latter happened very soon after the former.

Connie, I can't believe how much I've written. I didn't realize it—the keyboard has just been clattering as I sip. I will give you a break!

Forever,

Steve

I sent it; I sat there, bewildered and exhausted.

In telling her about Amy's resentments, I hadn't mentioned Lital—or Connie herself. Honesty was just an ideal, after all.

ConnieLn: Steve, Steve…

Yes it is all amazing and overwhelming.…

Please I hope you're not overdoing it with the wine. I understand that it must be so terribly hard because she's hinting about the big D with all that it means in your situation. Oh boy... She should talk to me about it. I know all about it—twice.

I'm thankful to you for telling me—for enabling me to find out, finally—about how it was for you after the breakup. At the same time it's almost unbearable for me to read it. I'm eternally grateful for your luck in finding Bob Sivers, and to Bob Sivers, for his helping you get through, and for his wonderful insight about pursuing the Jewish direction. I completely understand your cutting yourself off from the other kids because they couldn't understand you. I've been that way all my life, maybe to a less extreme extent, but not always.

But Steve, what I did—cutting you off suddenly and completely—was excessively and unnecessarily cruel; I still almost can't bear to think about it. You should know that since the time of my divorce I've been a member of a church, and that my cruelty at that time is one of the things for which I ask forgiveness.

Yes, I was hard hit too. At Oneonta there was a free psychological service for the students. They started me with a girl who was a trainee, an MA student in psych, but after one session—fortunately—she turned me over to her boss, a professor of psych and a psychiatrist, because of "suicidal ideation." I wouldn't be surprised if they were weighing whether to commit me. Instead he put me on antidepressants and "intensive therapy"—it was four times a week at the beginning. Steve, I don't have to tell you what pain is like. The guy, Dr. Ciapelli, did urge me—after a while—to make contact with you again. I couldn't—too shellshocked. I vowed that I would never again have a romantic involvement, that I would seek other things in life. I was then taking a course in art history, and I found that I loved it, and it gave me strength. In particular the older European paintings, with the Christian themes, did something for me. Most of all, the idea of a God who took suffering upon himself.

So you see Steve, even if our rivers were no longer flowing together, perhaps they were running parallel to each other?

So I ended up majoring in art history—to answer your question—and eventually got a BA in it. (And there it sits—as I'm now a pastoral brochure-writer.) As things turned out I never saw Winslow, but the Oneonta campus is very beautiful—up on a hill, with views of rolling hills and valleys—and that did something for me too, the crisp cool air up there, the incredible beauty especially in autumn. It was painful and uplifting at the same time in a way I can't explain, but you are one of the only people I've ever known who would understand what I mean.

Steve, it was not you who "caused" this, the crisis I was in. It was me—my being the way I was, too devastated within, unable to withstand anything.

I too became withdrawn at Oneonta, but maybe not as much. There were a couple of girls I got along with, and with one of them—Marie—I'm still in touch. So I had a bit of a social life. But I too backed out of the romantic game!—and it was not always easy since I had suitors, but I managed to keep them at bay.

Steve, when your father died—I almost wrote to you. I came very close to it. I was hit very hard by it. Just as you warned me, he hardly talked to me when I was there. But I knew how much he meant to you, and that he was a person with so much inside—because you told me and because I could sense it. What stopped me from writing to you in the end was the thought that it could lead to us getting back together again—and I was too scared of that, terrified of that, even though—if it hadn't been for my accursed fears—I certainly would have wanted it. And then, soon after that, I heard that you were with Amy. How did I feel? On one hand, tremendous relief—because it seemed to mean that you were all right, and you weren't alone. And on the other…why the hell didn't I write to him while I still could have? You see the deadly circle I was running through over and over again?

Oh boy, talk about clattering away—and I'm not even drinking anything, except mint tea. (My cat is making a ruckus for attention—with "Why does she keep clattering away like that?" looks.) My parents… Even after all this time, about the same. My mom is still in the same place on Beechwood Lane. She's been through rehab several times. Unfortunately it's always a sure thing that she'll return to it. As always, she has boyfriends, and they don't last long either. I tolerate her better now because I don't live there—I can tolerate her (even that not always) on the phone once or twice a week. You just have to prepare yourself that it's all going to be about her—the "terms" are that you're a satellite revolving around her and she has no ability to take an interest in you or relate to you.

And my father…still with his baby, his prize, the booming sporting-goods store in Cleveland. Still—him, too—going through relationships with people of the other sex like so many disposable plates and cups. Still gracing me with his once-a-year phone conversation and *even*…at longer intervals of course…a rare visit. I had sort of a scene—not really but a confrontation, a quiet confrontation—with him in Cleveland three years ago—but I'll save it for later! I'm writing so much here, soon I'll be able to submit it to publishers as a book!

Steve, Steve. I'm going to send you these ramblings, and you know what I hope? That you won't see them for a few hours, because you'll be asleep. I want you—at least for what's left of your night over there—to get a good night's sleep! Steve,

I truly understand the stress and the burden that you're under. Try to hang onto good habits! It helps!

Connie

S-Sandor: Connie, I want to hug you and kiss you.

ConnieLn: Steve, can I ask you a question?

S-Sandor: Shoot.

ConnieLn: When you wrote that, were you thinking of something? Did you have an image in your mind?

S-Sandor: Yes. 17-year-old Connie.

ConnieLn: Exactly. Just as I thought. I'm sorry to inform you that I'm no longer her. I'm not an old hag. I try to take care of myself. I don't think I look bad. But I am most definitely not 17.

S-Sandor: Send a picture.

ConnieLn: I'm not going to do that, Steve. You see, this is exactly what I was worried about. It was a couple of days ago that I came upon your article with your email address at the end. But as you see I didn't write to you right away. I waffled. The desire to do it was huge. On the other hand, to the best of my knowledge you were married, and I did not—did *not*—want to be the "former girlfriend" who comes into the life of the married man to stir up trouble. I will not play that role. Will not. Even *less* will I play that role now that I know that, unfortunately, your marriage may not be on a sure footing at this point. I will not play a destructive role, Steve.

S-Sandor: I can't even know what you look like?

ConnieLn: No.

S-Sandor: Wow, that good?

ConnieLn: Cut it out, Steve. It's probably not that good. You might think, wow, what a disappointment, she ain't what she used to be. But I really don't know. I'm not taking a chance.

ConnieLn: A chance that you'll think it *is* good.

S-Sandor: I really don't want to divorce. After Amy's been "cold to me" for so long, I can't say my feeling toward her is what it once was. But it could revive. I want to keep living with the kids.

ConnieLn: I know that, Steve. It's because of who you are.

S-Sandor: Yeah, for better or worse…

ConnieLn: What happened—after your father died you started up with Amy?

S-Sandor: In the days right after he died, she was with us, helping with things. I had never reacted to her before—she was just Nellie's friend, from the time they were in kindergarten I think. Too close to Nellie I guess. Now, I guess, I saw her in a different light—as a person in herself. I went bonkers. It was strange, because since the breakup with you, I hadn't reacted to any girl, except in the routine way that guys react to girls, and I wasn't sure I'd ever have a more serious reaction again. Now I went bonkers for Amy. Yet, even then, the feeling toward you never changed.

ConnieLn: So it started while you were still at Winslow?

S-Sandor: Yeah, at that point I, and Nellie too, came home from our colleges on weekends a lot to help my mother, who needed a lot of help at that point. Amy was there—going to Albany State and living at home. So it started. The logistics were difficult—where??—but we managed.

ConnieLn: I'm sure.

S-Sandor: So Connie, now you know the broad outlines of the S-Sandor story—we moved to Israel, we had a couple of kids, I started spewing articles around the Internet, my marriage started to falter. What about you? Your turn. What happened after Oneonta? Divorced plus child. How did it happen? Shoot.

ConnieLn: Oh Steve, I feel I'm corrupting you if I go into that now. I want you to get some sleep.

S-Sandor: Connie, I'm already corrupt and I'm not ready to get to sleep now.

ConnieLn: Oh, boy… OK. My cat is still acting like a neglected child (I can recognize the symptoms), there are tissues all over the place, but here goes.

When I got my BA, I knew it just meant I could teach art in schools, which didn't appeal to me. I was ambivalent about going for the MA, which was just more of the same. So I went home. I figured that, now I was older, I'd be able to handle my mother better, put my foot down when it was needed, be less sensitive to her. It was true but only up to a point. The other thing was, I felt sorry for her. I knew that—strangely enough—she liked it better when I was there, didn't like being alone.

I found a job selling ladies' clothes at the mall that was then going up in Renford Park. Aside from the money, it was good because I didn't have to be in the house with her much. Do you remember my cousin Liza? She was living in Schenectady then. She invited me to come see a jazz trumpeter one night at the Van Dyke's restaurant in Schenectady. She knew him from college—it was years before that because they were both beyond college age at that time. His name was Pat Winton and he was really good. He'd been touring for a few years with the Woody Herman band—all over the world. He was so good that Woody Herman gave him a lot of solos. The whole band had just played in, I think, Utica, and he and a few of his friends from the band had gotten a gig for one night at the Van Dyke.

I didn't know much about jazz but, sitting there with Liza, I was very taken with it—with the whole thing, and with him in particular. Do you know the song "It Never Entered My Mind"? He did a long, kind of introverted solo on that, and… well, it did me in. The only other time I'd sensed such depth in a man was—with you (and you weren't exactly a man yet when I already started to sense it). So during a break he comes over to our table and talks with us. I'm thinking—Connie, what about your vow? But my vow went out the window—I was quite amazed—and something started between us. It turned out that when he wasn't touring he was based in Des Moines where he grew up, and he invited me to come and visit him in Des Moines. So, I did.

He told me he hated the touring life, the pressures, and said he was quitting the band and asked me to come and live with him in Des Moines. After a couple more visits, I did that, too. He found me the job at the Parks Department. Pat and a group he was leading had a steady weekend gig at the most popular watering hole in Des Moines, and he taught trumpet to private students. There were a lot of squeals and screeches in our house from apprentice trumpet players. Pretty soon we got married. When I was 24 I got pregnant. One Saturday morning very early—I was a few weeks pregnant—I got a call from the police department. Pat was there. He'd been caught during the night going to a prostitute, and been arrested. They said I could come down and pick him up if I could come up with a thousand dollars' bail. I did my wifely duty.

It turned out he'd been doing it all the time. There was—you can imagine—a scene in the house when we got home. He'd been doing it after gigs. It was a habit that had started when he was touring. After gigs he'd feel these terrible pressures—that he'd played badly, that after devoting his life to the trumpet he couldn't play it at all—and this was how he dealt with the pressures. He assumed that, once he'd stopped touring, and—especially—once he was settled down and married, it would stop. But it didn't. Actually those weekend gigs at the bar were even rougher on him, because he was leading a small group, it was a more intimate setting, he was more in the spotlight, and even though I think very few of the drunks were thinking—if anything—wow, that guy really can't play, if anything they were thinking the opposite, well…artists are crazy. So he went and found his solace. I knew he was hanging out late after the gigs and coming home very late, but he told me he was going to bars with the guys in the group to unwind after the gigs, and though I wasn't crazy about it I never— never—suspected he wasn't telling the truth. Never dreamed in my wildest, wildest imagination—even though my life had had its ups and downs—what he was actually doing.

I won't describe to you the scene that morning. He wanted me to take him back and give him another chance but I wouldn't hear it. I told him I was contacting a lawyer ASAP and we were getting divorced ASAP, and that was exactly what happened. The whole thing took a few weeks. I let him keep living there for those weeks, but we were on different floors and I barely talked to him except about "business." What was my mental state? I wanted to do that thing again that I'd tried to do when I was a kid, and—horrifying as this might be—I actually think I would have if I hadn't been pregnant. Possibly feeling sorry for my mother would have stopped me, but being pregnant made it definitely out of the question. I didn't want to take the therapy route again. Instead I went to the nearest Catholic church—I didn't have time to shop around—and joined it. There are parental figures in Catholicism, there are images and themes of solace. I asked myself—do I really believe in all this? I really wasn't sure, but I thought—if it helps me, why not go with it, what difference does it make. Those themes and images had been instilled in me in early childhood, and they were still there, still alive. So I went with it, and it did help, along with—even more—the fact that I was now responsible for another life, not just my own. But I wouldn't say the uterine environment for Benny was the best. I wasn't in a wonderful mental state in those months—I was surviving. When I bore Benny a new friend of mine from the church— Alice—came to be by my side; there was no one else.

So, Steve, that set the stage for the next 15 years. This time I not only vowed to have no more romantic involvements, I etched it in stone, and for 15 years I've stuck with it, and I'm intending to stick with it for however many more years. Pat has remarried, lives not far away, and has two kids, a girl and a boy, so at least Benny—unlike his mom—has siblings, though I wouldn't say his connection with them is the greatest at this point. Pat has turned out to be quite a decent ex-husband—he pays child support faithfully, he takes Benny on weekends (but it's fewer and fewer weekends now because Benny has his own things to do), and he cares about him. Pat is not a bad guy, he just had a horrible habit. Whether or not he still has it, I have no idea of course; for his wife's sake I hope not. None of this— having two parents who at least care about him even if they're not together—appears to have helped Benny in particular. But that's the one subject I truly want to avoid, at least for now, so I can stay in reasonably good enough spirits to have this email exchange.

By the way, I'm in the "pro-Israel camp" in my church. There is, unfortunately, a group of people who are "pro-Pal-estinian." That means that they're always knocking Israel, de-scribing it as this dark terrible country, encouraging people to boycott it, taking trips to the West Bank to get the party line from Fatah people, etc. I've never been a very political person, but I knew that you were in Israel and I didn't like what I was hearing. Most of all, I didn't think it could be true if *you* had chosen to go and live there. So I've educated myself a little—reading opinion articles by people who are more balanced, like the columnist George Will if you know him. So I'm in the pro-Israel faction in the congregation, trying to present a different view from that of the pro-Palestinian bunch. That doesn't mean, of course, that I have even a scintilla of the knowledge that you have!

I am of course pro-everybody, I hope for the best, but I don't like to see Israel getting bashed like that.

Steve, are you still there?

S-Sandor: Yes, I've read your amazing account and I'm here.

My God my God what terrible things Connie...

I'm a jazz buff. "It Never Entered My Mind" is a gorgeous song.

We have trouble with Lior too. He's four years younger than Benny so maybe it's more mild.

Connie you're the sweetest person on the face of the earth.

Connie there's an empty bottle and an empty glass standing on the table beside my computer. Empty empty empty...

Connie do you remember Lake George?

ConnieLn: Yes of course I remember Lake George. Steve, keep that bottle and that glass empty. Enough.

S-Sandor: Remember being on the other side of the raft, where no one else could see us, and looking out at the whole lake and feeling like we could swim all the way across it?

ConnieLn: Yes. Good thing we didn't try.

S-Sandor: Connie—such purity and innocence—lost? Possible to regain?

ConnieLn: Don't know Steve. Tend to pessimism.

S-Sandor: We can get it back.

ConnieLn: Stop it, married man.

S-Sandor: Want to tell me about that thing with your father?

ConnieLn: That thing with my father. That confrontation in Cleveland you mean?

S-Sandor: Yeah.

ConnieLn: Oh God…

S-Sandor: Tell me about it.

ConnieLn: Steve—sitting there with your empty bottle—at God knows what hour—this is what you want to hear?

S-Sandor: Yes. Then we'll be caught up with each other. With the big stuff. I think.

ConnieLn: You know what? All right. It's having kind of a cathartic effect to write these things down. But one condition.

S-Sandor: What's that.

ConnieLn: No refills.

S-Sandor: Check.

ConnieLn: OK. Cat has fortunately gone to sleep. Tissues lie scattered. Here goes. One more episode.

Actually it wasn't such a big deal. About three years ago he invited me to come to Cleveland, said he had something important to tell me. He paid for a hotel for me. He took me out to dinner and explained to me that he had a lot of holdings from his successful business, and his health wasn't too good (he was 67 then, a smoker and drinker with emphysema and other problems), and he told me he'd willed all his money—all of it—to me, so I shouldn't worry about things. I was courteous and distant as usual and I said thanks—though to tell the truth I hardly felt any gratitude, just wasn't capable of feeling it.

Then we were sitting in the car outside my hotel, and I said—just said it, amazing myself, because I said it calmly and without that much emotion, or maybe more accurately, without that much affect—I said, "How could you just abandon me as a kid? How could you do that?"

Steve, it was night and it was pretty dark in the car and maybe that helped me do it—that we couldn't see each other too well.

He sat there as if he was pondering what I said. He was taken aback.

He said, finally—I remember this pretty precisely—he said, "I was very angry at Mom. I guess I just associated you and her together."

I said, "Associated us together? You didn't know that I was a separate person? That I was a human being in my own right?"

He sat there some more. Then he said, "I'm sorry. It wasn't good."

Then he said, "Maybe we should talk more and see each other more."

I said, "Don't bother" and got out and closed the door.

I did this right after he told me he was willing me all the money, Steve. How insane is that?

According to my religion I'm supposed to forgive people. With others I make progress, but with him I can't even make progress. Sad, isn't it?

S-Sandor: It's sad, Connie, but it's understandable and you needed to say that to him finally. He needed to hear it, not that—I imagine—it does him any good. Have you been in touch since then?

ConnieLn: It's been the same—his annual, or slightly more frequent, phone calls. He hasn't said anything further about the will. When someday I get that inheritance—assuming I'm still going to get it—it will be with a feeling like getting dirty, but it'll help Benny and I'll have no choice but to take it.

S-Sandor: Connie, it's…four in the morning, wow. It's Tu Bishvat. A Jewish tree-planting holiday. During the day thousands, tens of thousands, of trees will be planted, many of them by kids, all over the country. In earliest earliest spring, with white and lavender almond blossoms soaking up gentle sun. It's beautiful, isn't it?

ConnieLn: It's gorgeous.

S-Sandor: You have to come here and see the land.

ConnieLn: Let's put that aside for now.

ConnieLn: Connie, it's dark and cold in here. Down the hall my wife is sleeping. She doesn't forbid it, but she prefers that I not sleep there. Downstairs in her room my daughter is sleeping. She thinks we're a stable, happy family. Out in the Galilee—he's on a class field trip, to plant trees—my son is sleeping. He has more inklings that something's going on, but I think he thinks we're a stable family, too. Sad, isn't it?

ConnieLn: It's sad, Steve. But maybe the kids are right and things will hold together. I very much hope so.

S-Sandor: Connie, why all the suffering? What's it for?

ConnieLn: I wish I knew, Steve.

S-Sandor: I know there are explanations. It's tied up with free will. It's necessary so we can arrive at meaning. Connie, outside in the street, stray cats are wandering around, freezing and starving, eating garbage if anything. Do they get something out of their suffering? Does it make them deeper or wiser? Does it make any sense?

ConnieLn: It doesn't, Steve.

S-Sandor: It seems like God is sloppy.

ConnieLn: It seems that way, Steve.

S-Sandor: Yet you go to church.

ConnieLn: Yes.

S-Sandor: Why?

ConnieLn: Because I believe in God.

S-Sandor: So how can you believe in him?

ConnieLn: I believe in him because people experience him. He's love.

S-Sandor: Have you experienced him?

ConnieLn: Not directly, but I would say indirectly.

S-Sandor: So the love doesn't extend to the people, the creatures, who need it most?

ConnieLn: It doesn't seem to, Steve, part of the time.

S-Sandor: So why worship a God like that?

ConnieLn: Because He's there. It's much better that He's there, even if it doesn't explain everything.

S-Sandor: Connie, would it offend you if I said that I love you very deeply?

ConnieLn: I love you very deeply too, Steve.

S-Sandor: Connie, how did I end up like this? I wanted to build a life in the Land of Israel—a happy, stable family for me, my wife, and my kids. Instead I'm sitting here at four in the morning, looking at an empty wine bottle and an empty glass. How did I get here?

ConnieLn: We need loads and loads of strength, Steve.

S-Sandor: I will fear no evil, for thou art with me.

ConnieLn: I'm not sure who that was directed to, but I am with you. I always have been and always will be.

S-Sandor: Do you know that my grandparents were shot to death like dogs or quarantined cattle?

ConnieLn: I know that, Steve. I love you.

December 1, 1995

13

Dark and cold. I had woken up. I was lying in a room. I did not know where it was.

Wherever it was, I'd have to get a couple more blankets. I was tightly wrapped in a quilt, yet cold, my throat sore, coughing. I had a headache too. I didn't quite know what was happening, but it was lousy. Lousy lousy lousy...

Slowly, consciousness swam back up from the deep. French Hill. I was in French Hill. My new rented apartment.

I lay without moving—except the shivering—as I remembered. Amy taking me to it in the car (which, under the terms, she would be keeping) yesterday evening.

Remembered her taking the elevator with me to the seventh, highest floor, where my apartment was. Remembered her standing in the living room, surveying it, making a couple of suggestions about how I could arrange the furniture better.

Remembered the embarrassed silence between us.

Then she said, "Bye."

I said, "Bye.

That was it. Sixteen years of marriage, almost twenty years together—the end. Finis. This was not "divorce," it was

175

"separation." Divorce was a procedure that would occur some months later at the rabbinate. This, though, was the real divorce—the end. In Hebrew the word for divorce comes from the word for "expel." Not all divorces are expulsions; sometimes it's by mutual agreement. This one was an expulsion—and I knew who was the expellee.

Until the end, until it became clear in about October that Amy had made up her mind, I had hoped for a different result—even though my once-fervent feelings for Amy had gone underground, and my fervent feelings for someone else—someone who lived seven thousand miles away and whom I never saw in the flesh—had very much revived. I had told Amy about being in touch with Connie again. I had admitted—it wasn't so much honesty as the fact that there was no point trying to hide the truth, not from Amy—that my strong feelings about Connie had always been there and still were, but I had also told Amy the same thing I'd always, honestly, told her: that my greatest desire was to be with her and the kids. I still don't think it was Amy's awareness of the renewed connection with Connie that decided the issue. Nor the fact that, in the spring, her mother had died, removing that preoccupation from her mind. She had simply been going in a direction, consistently, for a while.

If I had to be expelled to an apartment by myself, at least it was in French Hill. Back in our early days in Jerusalem, I'd often passed through French Hill on the way to the Hebrew University campus on Mount Scopus. I still passed through it sometimes because I still went to the campus sometimes to meet with professors whose works I was translating or editing. French Hill—a neighborhood in northern Jerusalem, about fifteen minutes by vehicle from the German Colony—has a simple, classical beauty: the gold stone of its buildings, the blue of its sky, the green of its pines. The seventh-story apartment

I'd found had a view that grazed the rooftops of French Hill and landed majestically on Mount Scopus.

Now, though, as I trudged into the living room, it wasn't a time for views. It was past four in the morning; I'd piled on sweaters but it was still cold, well beyond the coldest nights in the German Colony apartment. I flicked on the light. I saw the landlord's drab furniture; and boxes, and things that had spilled out of boxes—books, odds and ends. I saw the half-full wine bottle and the empty glass where I'd left them on the coffee table; now I understood why I had a headache, for which alcohol plus a mere three hours of sleep, plus cold, is a good recipe. My PC—faithful, transplanted—was on its table against a wall of the living room; it had seemed the logical place to put it, close to the coffee and snack supplies in the kitchen. I would get coffee, but first I wanted to check emails. As soon as the computer came on, emitting its weak light, I turned off the electric light; I didn't want to see my new abode so much.

I clicked on the icon of Connie's picture, which she had finally sent after a while. I always clicked on it first—and last—thing each day, and many times during the day.

The only thing more beautiful than Connie way back then was Connie now. The auburn hair was shorter, the green eyes more sober, the eyebrows as delicately arched. The photographer had caught her in a wonderful fraction of a second—a look at once reflective, vulnerable, and alert.

I stared; then checked my emails.

There was minor stuff; nothing from Connie. I summoned her address, wrote "Connie, you there?" and sent it.

Returning to the computer with a cup of steaming coffee, I knew that, while the caffeine would give me a spurt of false energy to counteract the wine and meager sleep, it could also worsen the headache. But I had Dexamol. I would get the balance right.

Still fighting off shivers from the cold, holding the hot cup, I saw there was already a reply from Connie.

ConnieLn: I'm here. You're at the new place? Have you slept at all?

S-Sandor: I'm at the new place, and I've slept three hours, and even that's a miracle. How's Benny?

ConnieLn: Like I told you he was suspended again for two days. So this morning he was supposed to go back to school, and I barely—barely—got him out of bed. The principal said that if he gets suspended once more—this was the third time—he gets suspended from the school altogether. Which means he'll be a high school dropout. But what difference does it make. With the grades he gets, no college will ever take him anyway.

S-Sandor: Oh, boy. Connie.

ConnieLn: How do you feel?

S-Sandor: I'll feel better when it's light out, when there's sunlight on the stones and the pine trees.

ConnieLn: How were the kids?

S-Sandor: Lior—even though he'd known about it since October—gave me a startled look and said "You're *leaving*?" I said "Yeah, I'll be 15 minutes away, we'll see each a lot." They were words that didn't land anywhere—drifted out the window. Gali can't grasp it—"Abba when are you coming back?" You don't know what to say. "I don't know Gali, we'll see!"

ConnieLn: I'm so sorry about this Steve. I was hoping to the end that she'd change her mind. Even though I sensed it was a pretty hopeless hope.

S-Sandor: For us at least there's a silver lining.

ConnieLn: What's the silver lining?

S-Sandor: The silver lining for us is—us.

ConnieLn: "Us" already exists.

S-Sandor: Yes, but now it can really exist.

ConnieLn: Has it occurred to you that there's a logistical problem?

S-Sandor: Yes, it's occurred to me. It's also occurred to me that I'm a freelancer, and I can live in Iowa part of the year. My clients can send files to a computer in Iowa as easily as to a computer in Jerusalem. I can live there part of the year, and you can visit here, and the rest of the time we'll be...like this—in touch every day, a lot every day. It's not ideal, but I think we've both reached an age where we don't look for things that are ideal.

ConnieLn: First we're together for I don't know how long, in Iowa, and then you leave and we're thousands of miles apart from each other again? I wouldn't be able to bear that. I wouldn't be able to bear you leaving. And I cannot come to visit, not with Benny being like he is.

S-Sandor: Benny can stay with Pat.

ConnieLn: No he can't, he can't Steve, not now. He either persecutes his brother and sister, especially Cindy, or he tries to get them to smoke grass. He can't stay there. And anyway these are just details. I told you that I'm through with that kind of thing. Maybe you thought I was just saying it because you were married. Well now you're definitely not married, or on the way to not being married, and I'm still saying it. I really hate that I have to hurt and disappoint you when you're already going through something like this. I wish you wouldn't make me do this.

S-Sandor: So you're like a nun?

ConnieLn: You can think of it that way if you want. Steve—you have to take things slow. You can't plan your whole future now. I think the present is enough for you to cope with now.

S-Sandor: Connie, I've already been "divorced" for over a year.

ConnieLn: OK. I understand that. There's a world of women out there. Women who live in Jerusalem, or at least in Israel, not at the other end of the world. So if that's what you want to do, you can start with that now. You're a free man.

S-Sandor: Yeah, Connie, and how's that going to work. When they realize, when they sense, soon enough, that I'm already in love with someone?

ConnieLn: So, Steve. I wrecked your marriage. Now I wreck your future too. You see why I had all those doubts before I emailed you last winter? Wish I'd listened to my inner voice.

S-Sandor: Connie, stop with the guilt. You didn't wreck my marriage. It was already going downhill. It was doomed.

ConnieLn: Even if that's true, Steve—and I'm not at all convinced of it—what about all the years before that, when she knew about how you felt about me? That didn't affect your marriage?

S-Sandor: Connie, we broke up and I couldn't get over you. That wasn't your doing. It was me. You didn't send vibes that said I had to feel that way.

S-Sandor: Connie, can I ask you something? Let's say I'm going out with women…let's say something serious—seemingly serious—starts with one of them. How would you feel then?

ConnieLn: I'm not going to love it, Steve, but what am I going to do. I'm not going to run your life and put restrictions on you from Iowa.

S-Sandor: And what if I don't want it? What if it's something I don't want?

ConnieLn: Like I said. I wrecked your life.

S-Sandor: No Connie, you didn't wreck my life. You wreck your own life.

ConnieLn: Steve, I'm a wrecked person. You have to get that through your head. Pat wrecked me. OK, I'm like a nun, think of it that way. A nun in a convent. Wrecked.

S-Sandor: Connie—damn it I have to get some Dexamol.

I got up from the chair, the legs scraping the floor. I took two Dexamol. I made my way in the dark, didn't want to see my new quarters.

I pulled up the chair again.

S-Sandor: Let's say I come to Des Moines for a week. No obligations of any kind. I'll stay in a hotel. We'll just meet and see what happens—if anything. Maybe nothing will. Maybe the chemistry isn't there anymore, maybe it just seems that way when we email. And after a week, I'm back here.

ConnieLn: Not a good idea, Steve.

S-Sandor: Why?

ConnieLn: Because maybe something will happen.

S-Sandor: Let me get this straight. The terms are, we never see each other, because something might happen. Did I get it right?

ConnieLn: You got it right.

S-Sandor: That's crazy, isn't it?

ConnieLn: Yes it's crazy. My life has been crazy. Give me a normal life and I'll be perfectly normal. Give me a life that's not crazy.

ConnieLn: Steve, let me tell you something. Let's say I venture out—I venture out from this wall I'm hiding behind— and something goes wrong. I'll feel suicidal. I have a son, not that I do him any good, and this is not a game I can play. I already played and I lost really badly. I cannot take chances.

S-Sandor: Connie, I'm not 18 years old. I don't smoke grass at all.

ConnieLn: That's a good lawyerly answer, those are good arguments lawyer. Steve please stop. I can't do this anymore. I've had a miserable day. I have *nothing nothing nothing* and now I'm arguing with you too. PLEASE STOP.

S-Sandor: Connie I'm sorry.

ConnieLn: I come into your life and I tie you up in knots and make trouble for you too. Welcome to the Connie Show. Nothing but trouble. *Trouble trouble trouble.* Please stop I CAN'T TAKE IT.

S-Sandor: Connie I'm so sorry. Want me to call?

ConnieLn: No you don't have to call, if you call I'd rather it not be at a time like this. Steve stop apologizing. *You* shouldn't be apologizing. Your wife just threw you out into some apartment. Jesus.

S-Sandor: What's miserable about the day you've had?

ConnieLn: Benny.

S-Sandor: Something else happen?

ConnieLn: What doesn't happen. He makes fun of me. Last night I told him not to come home late, and he says, "What would be late Mom?" And I said "You've got to get back to school tomorrow and I would think twelve would be late enough." And he says, "Twelve? Got it Mom, making a note of it. See you." And he walked out.

S-Sandor: And when did he come home?

ConnieLn: God knows.

S-Sandor: Connie I'm so sorry.

ConnieLn: And he keeps blaming me. Of course. As always.

S-Sandor: Blaming you for what?

ConnieLn: The same thing. Throwing his father out before he was born.

S-Sandor: *Throwing* him *out?* There was a reason for it.

ConnieLn: Yes, and I'm going to tell him that? I'm going to tell him his father was going to whores, that I was sharing my husband with whores? Pat and I have a story that we tell him—we just couldn't get along anymore, we couldn't live with each other anymore. Somehow Benny came up with the version, or maybe he senses, that it was I who threw Pat out. And you know what? Maybe he's right. Maybe I should have given Pat another chance. Maybe someone else, a more normal person, would have been capable of it.

S-Sandor: Connie Connie Connie. No no no. Pat may be a decent person like you say he is, but it's one of the most shocking stories I've ever heard—that he was doing that. I can't say one hundred percent but many many women would have done exactly what you did.

ConnieLn: Pregnant?

S-Sandor: Yes pregnant.

ConnieLn: Thanks for trying to help but you're saying things that aren't true.

S-Sandor: Connie it *is* true. *Is* true. How could you have gone near him after that, how could you have been anything but revolted by him? The fact that you were pregnant is what makes it so horrifying.

ConnieLn: Steve, what's going to happen to us?

S-Sandor: I don't know. I don't know.

ConnieLn: God what a day.

S-Sandor: You're probably worn out.

ConnieLn: Kind of. I was up half the night worried if he was coming home, worried—as always—about what the hell he was doing out there. Finally I just fell asleep, he hadn't come home, I don't even like to think what time it was. In the morning he was lying in his bed, zonked out, God knows what he was doing, what he was on. I told him "You have to get to school or you're going to get suspended for good." I had to say it over and over. I had to shout at him. Finally he says, "Yeah yeah Mom, I don't need you bitching at me first thing in the morning." But he would *never* have gone to school if I hadn't so-called bitched at him. Steve, I'm supposed to be a PR person. And I'm coming to work dead tired, with dark circles under my eyes, looking like crap. Feeling awful. Not able to concentrate. And it's been like this all week. I can't do this. I can't keep up like this.

S-Sandor: Connie you're making me say things I'm not supposed to say. I want to hug you so much.

ConnieLn: You think I don't want that? What do you think I am, crazy? You think I don't dream about that all the time?

S-Sandor: Connie, you're trying your best with him. You can't do any more than your best. What you can't control you can't control.

ConnieLn: Yeah, and do you know what kind of fears I have? If something horrible happens, is it going to console me that I couldn't control it? Steve I'm sorry. You caught me in a bad time. *You're* in a bad time and I'm just piling these things on you. I'm really sorry.

S-Sandor: Connie we're both in a bad time. What's happening to you is more acute. What's happening to me, I knew it was coming.

ConnieLn: Steve, whatever I do, whatever I say, you and Benny are the two most important people to me. You and Benny. And he's cruel to me, and you're kind to me. It's a big difference.

S-Sandor: But I make trouble for you too.

ConnieLn: I don't call it making trouble. We have things we're trying to work out. I'm sorry I called you a lawyer. I really didn't mean it. I'm sorry.

S-Sandor: Don't worry about it. Connie, if you were up half the night, and it sounds like it could have been more, maybe you should try to get some sleep, even though it's not late there yet. Where's Benny?

ConnieLn: He's out bowling with the gang. Sometimes on these bowling nights he comes home earlier. They bet on all the games and he usually wins because he's a great bowler. He likes to come home and brag about how much he won. Also they finagle a lot of beer so maybe he has less craving for his other damned substances.

S-Sandor: Connie, maybe you should try to get some sleep and just try, try to put it aside and make your mind a blank. I know it's a lot easier said than done, but it's worked for me sometimes. Just refuse to think about it, wall it out, tell it you'll think about it tomorrow.

ConnieLn: Steve, do you think we'll be all right?

S-Sandor: Yes. We'll be all right.

ConnieLn: I'm sorry about before. I can't cope with these questions now, it's just…too much for me.

S-Sandor: I know. It's all right.

ConnieLn: OK, I'm going to take your advice and just give this a try now. Just shut it out. Maybe I'm exhausted enough that it will work.

S-Sandor: That's good. Good decision.

ConnieLn: I don't like to leave you like this. It's…it's still the middle of the night there, and you're alone. God.

S-Sandor: Connie, really it's all right. In not much longer it'll start getting light. I'm looking forward to seeing this place—the outside, that is—in the daylight. Really I'll be all right.

ConnieLn: Really?

S-Sandor: Really.

ConnieLn: OK, well…I can't convince myself that you're all right.

S-Sandor: Connie I'm all right. Really I am. You can check on me whenever you want.

ConnieLn: OK. OK. So…goodnight. I guess it's goodnight.

S-Sandor: Goodnight. We'll be in touch. We can be in touch all the time now, whenever we want. It's a wonderful thing, isn't it?

ConnieLn: Yes it is. Wonderful. Goodnight Steve. Whatever I say Steve, I…

S-Sandor: I know, Connie. Me too.

ConnieLn: Goodnight.

S-Sandor: Goodnight.

I waited a bit—just in case she wanted to add something; but there was no more.

I exited email; I clicked on the icon.

I sat looking at her picture in the dark.

April 9, 1997

14

Morning. I sat at the window of my apartment, feet up on the sill, sipping coffee. Outside it was spring. The sky was a melting Mediterranean blue, the stones of the nearby buildings brightly lit, the farther buildings merging in soft gold as they sloped up to the vague grandeur of the campus on its hill. The Song of Songs describes this season in the Land of Israel: "…the winter is past, the rain is over and gone; / The flowers appear on the earth; the time of the singing of birds is come, and the voice of the turtle is heard in our land…." Though I couldn't have distinguished a turtle dove's voice from that of other doves, there was no missing the cooing of the doves and pigeons and the singing of birds, the flowers blooming in the courtyard below.

I was in a much better mood than on that December night I'd moved here sixteen months ago; I was almost cheerful. It was partly because, in checking emails, I'd glanced over yesterday's exchange with Prof. Eugene Moon. He was the same Gene, the science and math whiz who'd been my best friend, and chess partner, in elementary school until his family had moved away during sixth grade. I now understood—more than I had then—that I'd thereby lost what could have been my only close male friend in the high school years. Gene, too, had seen an article of mine with my email address at the end, and had emailed me out of the blue. He, too—like my other academic friend from childhood, Nellie—seemed to be proceeding through life without major hitches; he was a professor of molecular chemistry at Caltech, married with three kids. Because, I think, we still felt close—and at the same time, because the huge geographical distance made it easier—we'd been quite open with each other about our lives and the routes they'd taken.

He well remembered my father and was sad to learn that he'd died young. He recalled me telling him my father was unbeatable in chess; he disclosed that he'd hoped for some chance to play him, to test his mettle against him, which never came.

He also remembered Connie—as far back as fifth grade; I could only locate my earliest memories of her in seventh grade, when I was becoming ultra-aware of girls in general. In fifth grade Connie had transferred from her Catholic school—straight into Gene's class. He remembered her as shy, quiet, and pretty; he said she seemed "so sensitive you thought she'd break if you touched her." He said it "made sense" that I'd gotten involved with her; he recalled me as a guy who, while more outgoing than Connie, also had "a lot going on inside" that he couldn't easily express to people, so it stood to reason that things had eventually started up between us. He was a bit more mystified as to why—especially when I explained to him that I wasn't considered Jewish—I'd chosen to move to Israel. He said it looked to him like "a nasty tribal conflict over there that's not going to be solved for a while." I told him that I identified with the Jews, that I saw Israel as a miracle of rebirth and wanted to be part of it, and that the "conflict"—the surrounding culture's rejection of a Jewish state—was just something one had to live with and endure.

Connie had become something of an e-wife; just as I had with Amy when the marriage was in better shape, and making adjustments for the eight-hour time difference, I "talked" with Connie every day, reviewing the latest developments, sometimes going into deeper thoughts. (Occasionally we actually did talk—on the phone; though email seemed our more natural métier.) We remained, though, in the same limbo as sixteen months ago. It kept getting worse with Benny; having been ejected from the school last year already, the issue was no longer keeping him in school but keeping him out of jail. Connie had been able to establish one rule with him: no drug pushers calling her landline. It didn't make much difference since they just called Benny's cell phone. He was running errands for them, mostly finding them clients—in return for a cut of the merchandise as well as money. Other than that he wasn't working; Connie knew that, by maintaining him, she was maintaining all of his activities. Her priest told her that she had no choice and she shouldn't see herself as responsible.

Under these circumstances it was pointless to try to push "the issue" between me and Connie; she was already at or even over the limit of what she could contend with. Instead, itchy and restless, I checked out the online dating scene—then still something of a novelty, the more so for a tech-challenged person like me. My rule, upon which I easily reached agreement with myself, was that I would not do anything that could lead me away from Connie. That meant, to begin with, disqualifying single women; they were usually looking for something very serious. The best bet turned out to be women who were recently divorced; they were sometimes enjoying a mood of liberation and looking for "fun." In e-dialogues, in café meetings, I made clear that I "wasn't looking for anything serious"; I even told some of them about the woman, the former girlfriend, in the States and the situation I was in with her. This led to some interesting experiences; but I found that trying to keep things in check, to prevent feelings and hopes from growing, was difficult and could get messy; and more recently I'd been desisting from the whole thing. I mentioned it to Connie; her response, or nonresponse, was a kind of studied neutrality.

Meanwhile I'd—at last—resumed work on my novel, the one I'd started back then in the apartment Amy and I had shared in Renford Park. It turned out that even being an expellee had its upsides; I had more time, and the present apartment—most of all the perch by the window—was wonderful for writing, full of silent, patient air, better than the best café. It was no problem to take off an hour or two from my other work and work on it. And I no longer had to worry, of course, about Amy being around and picking up on feelings that the novel might be stirring in me. Ken and Stacy were still there, having waited faithfully in its pages for a decade and a half. But now, of course, Stacy was no longer a stand-in for someone who was lost, a way of clutching at wisps of her; she was a character based on someone who'd stepped back into reality. It was, in brief, complex—especially navigating between the parts of the story that were essentially memories, from the Steve-Connie territory, and the parts that were inventions, from the more difficult, volatile Ken-Stacy territory. To jump ahead, this novel, *Life on the Ledge with You*, was eventually published, but you probably haven't heard of it because it was a small publisher and sales were modest.

For such reasons—getting to like the apartment better, having time to work on the book, having an e-wife to share things with—being an expellee hadn't turned out to be as bad as it had seemed at first; and I'd add that, by the time of the expulsion, the old feeling toward Amy had already cooled for quite a while. That left Lior and Gali.

I took them every other weekend, and theoretically twice during each week, though Lior—with all sorts of other things to do—sometimes skipped the weekday visits. Or sometimes, instead of those weekday visits, I'd take one or both of them somewhere in the city. As far as we could tell, Gali seemed all right. A few months earlier, about a year after the separation, when she was going on eight years old, she'd opened a couple of serious conversations with Amy about what had happened. Amy had explained to her that I wouldn't be coming back to live with them. She said we hadn't been able to get along with each other anymore, and that to have a marriage, people had to get along with each other and have the right kind of feeling between them. Gali asked if I could just live in the study—we wouldn't be married, but I could live there. Amy said the study was too small, and that people couldn't really keep living together after they were divorced. Gali then said that she liked my apartment because it was high and you could watch the doves. Amy said that, though Gali sometimes seemed to sink into contemplative states, there was no sign—at home or at school—that anything was wrong. We hoped it would stay that way. I wondered if Gali had Nellie's forgiving nature that didn't take others to task.

There were, not surprisingly, more issues with Lior. His grades slacked off; he'd already had a history of behavior problems in school—clowning around in class, making sassy quips to teachers—and now it got worse. On a class trip, he and a couple of friends had some kind of ruckus at three in the morning and overturned a tent. Now, at age fourteen, he was starting to go out at night. Amy gave him time limits of eleven o'clock on weekdays and twelve o'clock on weekends; Lior sneered that the latter in particular was a joke, that none of his friends had to come home so "early"—which, unfortunately, had some truth to it, since there's an Israeli norm of giving kids a lot of freedom. On weekends in particular, he regularly came home after—though not drastically after—the deadline.

I held talks with him about these issues, but felt myself to be in a weak position. It would have been hard to imagine without actually becoming a divorced dad. Lior never said it outright, but you could feel it, almost palpable, in the air—this guy's telling me what to do and he couldn't even keep living with us.

It was true that Lior—so far at least—didn't seem to be in the Benny league. At fourteen Benny had already been skipping school a lot, going places and meeting people Connie didn't even want to know about. I couldn't help thinking, though, about Amy's brother Sammy, the drifter who had never straightened out. But it was too early to know.

As I was sitting there, contemplating the morning view, the phone rang. I'd set it up on a small table at the edge of the couch, and from where I was sitting I could take the receiver to where I sat by the window, which is what I did.

"Hello?"

"Steve?"

"Hi, Amy. How you doing?"

"OK. Is this too early?"

"No, not at all. I've been awake for a while."

"That's good. I had a little time before work today. So how you doing?"

"Me? Good… Work's going well. I've been working on my novel, too."

"That's the one…the same one?"

"Yeah. The old one. The one you didn't like me working on."

"The one with Stacy in it?"

"Yeah."

"So…it's resurrected?"

"Yeah. I've got more time these days, so I find I can sneak it in between my other work."

"So, back with Stacy. What's happening with the real Stacy?"

"The real Stacy?"

"The person she's kind of based on."

"I think you mean Connie."

"Yes."

"Well. We're very good e-friends. Close e-friends. We're in touch all the time."

"That's all?"

"Well, it's a long story. For now, yes. She's in a really difficult situation with her son."

"Well, that actually reminds me of the main reason I'm calling you."

"Oh?"

"You're meeting with Lior today?"

"Yeah. At four. Supposed to meet at the Ilanit café downtown."

"He's been saying some weird stuff lately."

"Yeah? Like what?"

"I don't know. He says he doesn't see why he has to live in Israel and why he has to serve in an army. He's got this plan of escaping to the States on his eighteenth birthday."

I sat silent.

"He hasn't said anything like that to me at all."

"Well, he says it to me. Maybe he doesn't want to say it to you."

"So… I would think that for you it's not such a bad thing that he's saying things like that."

"Actually, it is."

"It is?"

"Yeah. I don't want him leaving here."

"But then you and Gali—in a few years, when Gali's eighteen—could follow him. Fulfill your dream."

"No, Steve, that's not my dream. I wouldn't want that either."

I shifted in my chair. "I sort of got the impression, for a long time, that living here wasn't something you were crazy about."

"Well, I understand how you got that impression. Crazy about it, I don't know. But I think it's good."

"Yeah? Even that I wouldn't have thought."

"Steve, while we were together I wasn't sure what were your opinions or my opinions anymore. Your opinions are very strong and passionate. I'd think, do I really think this or am I being influenced? Now it's a little clearer."

"So you've been liberated."

"Yeah, Steve, I don't need sarcasm first thing in the morning. What I mean is that I wouldn't want Lior to leave, and not only because he'd be far away. And I wouldn't want to follow him there either."

"Yeah? Why's that?"

"Because it makes sense to be here. Back there my parents took me to a synagogue to try to drill the Jewish thing into my head. They may have succeeded, but I didn't like it, or I was ambivalent about it. Here it's natural. It's just who you are and it makes sense."

"It's kind of organic."

"Yeah, you could put it that way."

"Well, of course I agree with that. I wonder what would have happened if you'd had these revelations a few years ago."

"Steve, again, I'm not looking for little sarcastic digs. There were other issues. I think you know that."

"Yeah, of course. Guess there were. But Lior, you know, he's fourteen. At fourteen people say all kinds of things."

"I know. But he's saying it a lot and I don't like hearing it, and Gali's hearing it too. You don't want to talk to him about it?"

"No, I can talk to him about it. But I'm not sure he puts much stock in what I say."

"Why would you think that?"

"Oh…it's a feeling I get. I kind of get a vibe from him—and I really don't blame him, what the hell does he understand—a vibe as if I'm someone who's invalidated himself, couldn't stick it out and live with his family."

"Funny you should say that because I don't get that impression at all. I get the impression he really respects and looks up to you."

"Really?"

"Yes."

"That's the impression you get?"

"Yes."

"Funny because I don't feel that when I'm with him."

"Well, Steve, what can I say. I don't know how people get the impressions that they get. You could write a book about it. So you'll talk to him?"

"Yeah, I'll give it a try. What the hell. Can't promise anything. I'll give it a try."

"Good. And you'll let me know how it went? By email or whatever?"

"Yeah. I'll let you know."

"Good. Thanks."

"Sure... So how's it going otherwise?"

"Oh, not bad. My father has a new girlfriend already."

"Yeah?"

"Sammy and Rina have met her and they say she's kind of weird. But my father's kind of weird too. So maybe it's a good match."

"Ha-ha. Yeah, that could be."

"I really should get going now."

"OK. Take it easy."

"You too. Have fun with your e-friend."

"Oh. Yeah, I will."

"Bye."

"Bye."

I kept sitting there, holding the receiver, until it started making unbearable noises.

15

The Ben Yehuda Street pedestrian mall is the heart of commercial Jerusalem. Locals and tourists mill about. Hebrew and English predominate but you hear many other tongues too. Endless shops sell Judaica, knickknacks, T-shirts. Buskers play guitars, clarinets, karaoke keyboards, and whatever else. Also much in evidence are falafel and ice cream joints, here and there interrupted by a café or even a restaurant. Outside one of these cafes, Lior stood waiting for me.

Lior had blue eyes and my father's dark, curly hair. At fourteen he had a flushed, acne-strewn face, a look as if he were seriously mulling something. Like my father and unlike my father's kids, he had strong talents in the science and math direction; in elementary school he'd excelled in those subjects and had particularly loved science projects. Now, though, his grades in all subjects were falling off.

As I mentioned, like immigrants in Israel generally, we mostly spoke the "old" language with the kids. Lior's Hebrew-accented English was quite good, enhanced by watching current American TV shows.

"Hi, Abba," he said.

"Lior, what's doing," I said, unsure whether to clap him on the back or shake his hand, settling for the latter.

"You hungry?" I said.

"Uh, yeah yeah, OK."

We sat at a table by the window; the café was crowded and noisy. A waitress—a dark, demure Israeli beauty—approached, tried to assess us as Hebrew or English speakers, and ventured a "Hello, how are you?" in English. I replied in American-accented Hebrew that we were doing fine and asked for menus.

"So," I said to Lior, "how you doing?"

He was sitting with the busy walkway of the mall outside the window to his right, and he glanced in that direction frequently. There was indeed much to see there—not least the girls in the warm April afternoon—but Lior, at that age, also had a habit of tossing glances over his right shoulder.

"I'm OK, Abba," he said. "Write that article?"

"Uh…what article?"

"Last time I was over there, you told me you had to finish some article by, you know, one in the morning, ha-ha."

"Oh. Yeah, yeah, I wrote it, I sent it to them about one, said, hope this is OK."

"Ha-ha! Anyone can just send stuff to those websites?"

"No, not really. Lots of people send them stuff, but they pick the stuff that they like."

"They like your stuff?"

"Yeah. Guess so."

"They pay you for it?"

"Yeah. Not a hell of a lot, but it helps."

The waitress came back with our menus—the Hebrew, not English edition.

We sat scanning them somberly.

"I'm gonna get the *kubeh*," Lior said.

"Good."

I—a vegetarian, and impatient with menus—ordered humus with *pitot* and French fries; Lior asked for somewhat more elaborate fare centering on *kubeh*. The waitress collected the menus and walked off; Lior shrugged out of the light jacket he'd worn to school so that it hung from the chair behind him.

"So," I said, "you got two more months of school?"

"Hah, yeah."

"Getting hard to concentrate these days?"

"Ha-ha, yeah."

"Hey, you used to be quite an ace."

"What, at school?"

"Yeah."

"Yeah. Used to be, ha-ha."

"We should keep those grades in the pass column, though."

"Oh, Ema tell you about that?"

"Yeah."

"Hey, I don't know what she's telling you. They're in the pass column."

"She said history might be dipping out of the pass territory, into the other territory."

"Ha-ha! The teacher, you know, she's real boring. She stands there at the board and she like, writes things, and then she points at what she wrote there and she tells you what it is, in this like tiny voice that you can hardly hear, ha-ha."

"Yeah, what can you do. You have to deal with boring teachers sometimes. You have to deal with all kinds of people."

We both fell silent, as if I'd said something taboo; Lior glanced over his right shoulder, seemed to focus on something, squinting.

His cell phone rang. "Ido!" he said. "*Ma inyanim?*"

He sat grinning and hunched, talking and guffawing.

I heard him say, "I'm here with my father. Catch you later."

"That's Ido," he told me. "He's getting a new amp for his guitar. Really, really powerful."

"I hope it won't drive his parents crazy."

"Ha-ha! No that's when, when he works out with his band—works out?"

"'Practices' is better."

"When he practices with his band, that's when they turn them up loud. When he's, like, practicing at home, he keeps it so it won't drive everyone crazy. Ha-ha!"

"Well, that's good."

"Hey, I really like that CD I borrowed from you. Sonny Rollins."

"Oh, you like that?"

"Yeah, it's got like…energy. Wow."

"We saw him once in Massachusetts. It was incredible."

"Fantastic. It's like…got such energy."

"I like his calypso numbers best. There's one on that disc I gave you—'Don't Stop the Carnival.'"

"Oh yeah, that's great. I'm like listening to that and… wow! Nirvana!"

The waitress came with our food. She spoke to Lior in Hebrew, to me—having heard my accent—in English. Thinking an immigrant wants to be addressed in his native tongue, not in the language he's learned, is a common error.

We sat there eating studiously, Lior glancing over his shoulder. Next to us, at a long table, a group of American Christian tourists were talking loudly about the Sea of Galilee.

"So," I said, "I'm hearing you want to get the hell out of this place."

He looked at me, slightly surprised, uncertain.

"Oh, wow. Bet Ema told you about that, too."

"Well, you could say I heard it through the grapevine."

"Oh, wow, I can't talk in that place anymore. It's like, they've got it bugged, ha-ha!"

"Hey, what do you think Ema and I are going to talk about, if not you guys."

"Yeah? That's what you and Ema talk about?"

"Yeah, pretty much."

"Ha-ha. Yeah, Abba I don't know. I'm not sure why I've gotta live in the craziest place in the world. Buses blowing up in the streets and all that."

"The terrorism's gone way down since Netanyahu was elected."

"Yeah but like, when you're eighteen, you gotta go in the army. There's always something."

"It's a rough area."

"Yeah, but like, Rachel and Debbie, when they're eighteen, they don't have to go into the army, they can go straight into college. I mean, like, they're girls, but here even the girls go into the army. I don't wanna, you know, waste three years running around like that. Just because our government and some other government say, OK, we're gonna have a war, I don't wanna have to go to a war because of that."

"Well, I disagree with all of that. OK if I say why?"

"Sure. You're the one who's writing all the articles. Look out, I'm gonna get slaughtered, ha-ha."

"OK. First of all, you don't necessarily have to be *kravi*.[2] There are more than enough volunteers for *kravi* and you probably wouldn't be forced to be. Also, they need guys like you— guys who are good in the science and math direction—for important *lo kravi*[3] jobs, like in intelligence and computers

---

[2] "Combat," meaning "a combat soldier."
[3] "Noncombat."

and all that. You can do a lot without being *kravi* if you really don't want to be."

"Yeah, but it's three years of my life."

"Second, as you know, I've served in Tzahal[4] quite a lot, and I'm really glad I have. A lot of it is actually fun. You might be surprised, and you've probably heard about it, but a lot of army life is fun. And I've been able to experience all kinds of things. I've learned a lot from it. Parts of it have been hard, yeah, but what I've done in the army—I wouldn't give up for the world."

"Yeah, but you can learn and learn until like, you know, a bullet lands in your head, ha-ha. You see guys walking around here with, like, one arm, one leg. I don't wanna be one of them."

"Lior, can I ask you something?"

"Yeah, sure."

"Let's say there's an earthquake in Jerusalem. A big earthquake. Buildings crashing down, thousands of people homeless, walking around in the streets, lost all their possessions. Would you want people outside of Jerusalem—people in Tel Aviv, in Haifa, wherever—to care about it? Would you want them to help?"

"Yeah, sure."

"So people are connected to each other? If there's some kind of disaster in Tel Aviv, should we in Jerusalem help them?"

"Yeah, OK. Yeah, we should."

"So it's not just everybody for himself, everybody looking out for himself. That's what an army is. If it weren't for Tzahal, there'd be a big disaster here. Not just in Jerusalem or in Tel Aviv, but all over the country. You're helping other people be

---

[4] Hebrew acronym for "IDF," Israel Defense Forces.

safe. You're helping other people survive. It's not that our government wants wars, or that our people want wars. I think you probably know that about us, that we don't want them. But sometimes you have to defend yourself, and other people too. That's what you do by serving in Tzahal. You're helping people."

"Yeah, but in America you don't have to serve in the army. It's, like, only volunteers."

"Well, America's a much bigger country. And here there's more of a security problem. This is a rougher part of the world."

"Yeah, Abba, that's just it. Like, why do I have to live out here with all these crazy people, guys blowing up buses, crazy preachers like they got in Gaza telling people to go blow themselves up. Like, that's not me. That's not me, I'm not part of that."

"So you're part of America?"

"Well, I can get to be part of America."

"You know, America's targeted by all kinds of terrorist organizations, too. Let's say America starts getting hit by terrorist attacks. Let's say they start drafting people into the army again. So, then where you going to go? Australia?"

"Australia's got great beaches, ha-ha."

"No, really, it's like I said before. It can't just be every man for himself. What are you saying—'I'm with you guys, but if it gets rough, I'm out of here?' Then you're not really with anybody. Then you don't belong to anything."

We both fell silent.

Finally he said, "Well, I can take my chances with America. Maybe that stuff won't happen over there."

"Yeah, and you know what the Israelis do over there? There are studies on this. They just socialize with other Israelis and speak Hebrew with them, and they never really assimilate into America. They stay there for years, and they never really feel part of America, and after a while they feel they've made a mistake, but by then it's too late because they're tangled up in jobs and things. A big study of this just came out."

"Yeah, my friend Natan's got an uncle kind of like that. Been in Miami, I don't know, fifteen years, wants to come back here but he can't anymore because he can't find a good enough job here or something like that, ha-ha."

"Once they're over there they start to miss the things here that are special."

"Yeah, like what? What do we got that's special?"

"Well, we've got us. We're the only people who are just like us. There's a lot that's really unique here. It's the only country that people came back to after so many years. It's the only Jewish one. It's the only one that speaks Hebrew. It's a young country and we're building it. We're building something new together—and it's old at the same time. That's a unique situation in the world. Yeah, I know, there are people who aren't part of it so much—geez, if I only had a Green Card. But for the people who are part of it, who care about it, it really is special. The situation with the wars and terrorism is tough, but it makes us closer to each other, too."

"Yeah, Abba, I don't know, you hear the news on TV, and it's like, this scandal and that scandal, this corrupt politician and that corrupt politician, I don't see what's special about that."

"Lior, we're just people. There are going to keep being scandals and corrupt politicians because that's what there is wherever there are people. They have them in America, too, don't worry. But the news doesn't report it when people are nice to each other and help each other. There's a lot of that too, isn't there?"

"Oh, yeah. Like the other day, this woman, I think she was some kind of tourist, from Belgium or something, she fell down on King George Street, I think she like tripped over a curb, and all these people, they crowded around her, and they helped her, and they helped her stand up, and they like kept staying with her till they were sure she's all right. I'm thinking, like, wow, that's cool."

"Yeah, and that doesn't happen as much in a lot of places. We've got a lot that's special here, Lior. And another thing is, I'm here, and Ema's here, and Gali's here. Ema doesn't want to leave either. She might have wanted to once, but she doesn't anymore. So I don't know how you'd feel over there by yourself. I did it—I moved from one country to another, and it's not easy. It's not easy being far from my sister and my mother all the time. But I did it for a positive reason, because I wanted to be here, not to get away from there. If you just want to sort of escape and be by yourself over there, I don't know how that's going to work out for you."

"Yeah…it's like, here you gotta serve in the army and get shot in some war, and there you gotta live far away from everybody. Tough world. Ha-ha!"

"Well, think about it…. Want some dessert?"

June 18, 1997

16

NellS: Hi, Steve. I'm taking my midday break here in my office, and I was wondering how you're doing. I feel that if I could just get over this hurdle—all the final papers I have to grade—I might make it to some semblance of the summer vacation that's supposedly awaiting me. Our good news is that it looks—we have it on good authority—as if Joel's promotion to full professor is clinched. Once it's "official" we're going to hold a little celebration at our place; Joel has wanted this for so long and worked so hard for it. It would be great if you could come to that!—not easily accomplished, I know. And my dream is that the summer will actually give me enough peace and quiet to get serious work done on my book on Verlaine—*si seulement....*

So how are you doing? How's Lior? I've been getting somewhat more upbeat reports from Amy and I was wondering what your impression is. And how's your novel going? I envy your ability to work relentlessly on it even when you have a lot of other work to do! I'm hoping I'll yet develop that ability, somehow. And, finally—there, now I've overloaded you with questions—how's it going with Connie? Any developments?

Nell

S-Sandor: Hi, Nellie. Good timing—it's evening here in French Hill, dark and quiet outside, and I was just taking a break from work myself. Or maybe not that much in the mood for it.

How am I doing? What can I say, Nellie. It's toughest at this hour. Over at the old place the TV's on, Gali's getting ready for bed...what can I say. In the morning I'll walk out into the French Hill sunlight, with the smell of the pines and the blue sky, and I'll feel—again—that in the end it's all benign. It's how morning makes me feel—might as well make the most of it.

Send my *mazal tov* to Joel! Yeah, it would be great if I could make it to the celebration. Complications are—Mom and Ed want to come *here* pretty soon, maybe in July, so there's the redundancy problem; and my work schedule as usual. But once you've got it planned, let me know and I'll see.

Yes, with Lior things look better lately, I'm happy—though with due caution—to say. He seems to be doing his homework again, and it looks as if he's finishing the school year with pretty decent grades, except maybe in history, but it appears that at least he's not flunking that. Amy says he also stopped talking about leaving Israel. I had a talk with him a couple of months ago, and though I'm cautious about taking credit, the improvement seemed to start around that time. Hope it keeps up, and that the effect won't wear off, if that's what it was. On the other hand, he keeps staying out till late hours, but it's kind of a general plague around here. It may bother us more because we have distant memories of parents telling us to come home at some outrageously restrictive hour like eleven—unthinkable around here, at least on weekends.

Yeah, my novel's progressing. Whether it's going to lead to anything, like eventually getting published, is an open question of course. The fact that I have an easily discoverable online track record of published articles that can be considered "right-wing" or "conservative" is actually more likely to be a detriment than an advantage. And as for how I manage to keep working on it amid all my other work, one of my secret methods is that, as the time I've allotted for novel-writing begins, I drink a strong coffee—to the point of hyperactivity and not being able *not* to write. A tip, for what's it worth—though I suspect that with the kind of writing you're doing, having to incorporate a lot of sources and notes, being hyper would actually not be helpful.

And…Connie. Oy. What I mean by that is oy for her and oy for me. Oy for her because the situation with her son keeps being dreadful. The latest is that he's talking about moving out—moving into an apartment in Des Moines with some of his very problematic "friends." Connie admits that it would be a relief to have him out of there, but also fears the aloneness—and fears losing whatever last shreds of restraint might still exist.

Oy me for because I'm pretty much stuck in this state of affairs—Connie as very close friend, Connie as needing me very much and not really wanting me to look for anyone else, but still being unable to go beyond this platonic e-intimacy we now have. Stuck here because I, too, don't want to look for anything else and risk losing her—losing her as a mate—a second time, while also realizing that this isn't really a full-fledged life I'm living now.

NellS: Do you tell her this is how you feel?

S-Sandor: I hint at it, and sometimes I raise it more explicitly though gingerly, and her answer is the same—I can't. And there's a reluctance to keep burdening her with this issue when she's already so burdened.

NellS: First of all, Steve, I want to say how happy I am to get this confirmation that things seem better with Lior! He's such a sweet kid and I so much hope that the positive trend will continue. He's lucky to have you for a dad!

Now on the other thing, the Connie issue, let me be honest with you—let me be less nice to you, perhaps—and say that from a rational standpoint it's hard to understand what you're doing. Even under the best of circumstances—that Connie would feel herself to be capable of a relationship—she lives in Iowa, she works a job that gives her a couple weeks' vacation a year, she has a problematic son with whom, unfortunately, a crisis could erupt at any time. You, meanwhile, are a person identified with the Jews who's deeply committed to living in Israel. You haven't seen Connie for—what is it now, 25 years?—and meanwhile there's a dating scene around you for divorced and single people—real live women who live where you live! That this e-friendship between you and her is deep and genuine I don't doubt for a second. That you should sacrifice so much—maybe even the possibility of a better life—to this hope of it turning into something else, which still hasn't happened even after you've been divorced for a year and a half…I don't know.

S-Sandor: Nellie, there is no other woman for me than Connie. Something happened to me when I was 16—on that first night I was with her—and it has never changed. Wasn't my marriage, my failed marriage, a lesson in that reality? I loved, liked, and was attracted to Amy, but Connie, the thought of her, was always there, and never went away—until she actually did come back. Why should I get something started with another woman when that's the case—and all the more so now that I'm in touch with Connie every day? The other woman isn't going to sense that my heart isn't really with her?

And as for the logistical issue, it's tough but it's not pro-
hibitive. Yes, I'm deeply committed to living in Israel, but I
don't have to live here all year round—as a freelancer I can live
in Iowa part of the year, and conduct my business from a computer there the same as from a computer in Jerusalem. Connie,
it's true, is tied to her job, and to her son and his problems—but
not totally because her ex-husband lives in Des Moines, and if
she were visiting here, and something came up with Benny, he
could handle it. And the other thing is—Connie is now, like
me, 43, and in 12 years she can retire from her job with a good
pension. At that point she's not necessarily tied to Iowa.

NellS: Ah, so you win in the end. Everybody's there with
you.

S-Sandor: Well, I don't know about everybody. If it's
Lior, Gali, and Connie--yeah, I'd call that winning.

NellS: Steve, let me say first of all that I understand you—
because I remember those times you had Connie over at our
house and what a sweet person, what an exceptionally sweet
person she was. Before that I'd just see her in school, and I only
knew that one terrible thing about her. But even though she
was quiet and shy around us and talked little, I'd think—my
brother knows how to pick 'em. I never saw two people so
thrilled with each other (don't tell Joel I said that). So I can
understand that you couldn't get over her, and I can also understand how Amy felt about that. I understand both of you,
I'm full of sadness that it ended, and along with the sadness
I'm trying to arrive at some acceptance.

Connie, though—sweet, sensitive, and deep as she is—is
also a very wounded person, a very deeply wounded person.
It's funny the way we've come full circle to that conversation
that night—I don't know if you remember it, it was on the
night that Grandpa had the stroke—that conversation where

I told you I was worried that she might be trouble for you. In that regard, has anything changed since then? Meanwhile she's been through even more traumas. Do you want to take a chance with this again?—that something will go wrong, as it did the first time, and she'll again have an extreme reaction?

And Steve, your romanticism—your belief that this is an eternal love—is undoubtedly charming. But if I can just be the advocate of the devil, of cold rationalism—can you know that, if you do get around to seeing her again, it will be the same, that the "thrill" will still be there after 25 years? You're already talking about 12 years from now, when she retires—is this not putting the cart before the horse?

S-Sandor: Nellie, nothing's going to "go wrong"—if it does get started again. I'm not 18 years old. I wouldn't be that stupid.

NellS: Steve, I didn't meant that—of course you wouldn't do that. But who knows—maybe you'll be with her someplace and you'll look at another woman askance, or maybe you'll have some interaction with some woman related to work or whatever, and she'll go off the deep end again. She's not stable.

S-Sandor: No, Nellie, she's not a nutcase like that, not paranoiac. I've been corresponding intensively with her for two and a half years now, and I don't see anything like that. Yes, it's true that corresponding is not the same as finally encountering her in the flesh, that a whole lot of water has flowed under the bridge since 25 years ago, and that meanwhile she had another shock, a real bad one. So that is the one concession I'll make to what you're saying, to the god of cold probability and rational calculation: I should reencounter her before I make up my mind totally. I can tell you a few things already, though. That— as you would expect—the essential person who was there 25 years ago has not changed, has only sobered and mellowed beautifully; that this is so enchantingly evident in the pictures she's sent me that I can sit mesmerized by them for hours; that if you want "thrills," when she and I occasionally talk on the phone her voice—the sound of her voice—is a soft thrill that sweeps me into different worlds. So that is why, when I make a concession to cold calculation, I'm doing it with the iciest reasonableness I can muster; more intuitively I don't really doubt that I'll be as attracted to her as always. And meanwhile there is no point in going after others, in trying to start something with someone else, until I've at least had that reencounter with her—I can't do it.

And by the way—of course I remember that conversation that night; I remember everything about that crazy night. This does seem like a reprise, doesn't it.

NellS: Yes, it does. It makes sense that you remember the first instance, not least because you have such a good memory.

Anyway, Steve—you've made your case. Of course the romantic in me is rooting for you, rooting for you and her; though I wish I could say I could get rid of my misgivings. So, brass-tacks time: do you see any chance of her relenting? And how long are you willing to keep trying and hoping like this, to be in this limbo?

S-Sandor: "Will I wait a lonely lifetime? If you want me to I will." I don't know about a lonely lifetime, but those words came to mind. Connie's going through changes. Things keep getting worse with her son, and now he may be moving out. I don't know how that would affect her. Sometime ago she said that she dreams of being hugged by me; it was when she was agitated and she let it slip out. It ain't easy but I can take it slow for now. For the time being at least, I would rather be in this intense e-friendship, whatever the hell one calls it, with Connie than in a "real" relationship with some other woman—it may sound crazy but that's how it is. I'm not saying it can go on like this forever. But I don't "always hear time's wingèd chariot hurrying near"—it's not at that point yet.

NellS: To go with the Beatles again, if she dreams of being hugged by you, "you know that can't be bad." But still, it could just be dreams. She's a religious Catholic, isn't she? I would think the Holy Land has some pull.

S-Sandor: Yes, Nellie, it's been one of my blandishments. It definitely resonates with her. All the more so because of her distress.

NellS: Well, Steve, over here in my relatively orderly, prosaic life, I should stop putting off the inevitable—returning to paper-grading. Thanks for filling me in—I was wondering. It's a complicated situation for sure. Do keep me updated!

S-Sandor: Sure, I'll do that. Speaking of religion, though... can I mention one more thing?

NellS: Sure.

S-Sandor: You might remember that sometime back we talked about me and the conversion issue, about why I never converted to Judaism. Lately I've been having the thought—which may actually be an insight, not just a thought—that the real reason was...Connie.

NellS: You mean that you wouldn't be able to marry her someday?

S-Sandor: No, not so much that. There are ways to get around that if it's what you really want to do. No, something more...symbolic maybe. That converting would have meant greater distance from her. As if it would have meant—or at least I felt it to mean—closing a door behind me, putting myself within the Jewish space, and even the Israeli space, in a way that would be closed off to her. I don't know, it makes sense only on a symbolic level.

NellS: Yes, it makes a certain sense, Steve, and I'm sure that this thought doesn't arise out of nowhere. When you used to tell me that the reason was alienation from religion, or not wanting to submit to rabbis, I didn't feel totally persuaded. You've been a deeply torn person.

S-Sandor: Yes, I have, but I'll say this in my defense: that way back when I started with Amy, I did not think it would be this way. I thought I would make the transition from one woman to another, as people usually are able to do.

NellS: Steve, that night when you came back from being with Connie for the first time, there was something changed about you, something rapt about you.

S-Sandor: And I've been rapt ever since. Wrapped. Well, things are now as they are.

NellS: Yes, they are. I can only say that I'll be waiting for updates.

S-Sandor: OK, Nellie, you'll be getting them. Bye for now.

NellS: Bye.

July 22, 1997

17

My eyes opened. I knew I was awake for good—whether or not I'd really slept enough.

Pitch dark. I peered at the clock on the night table. Just past 4 a.m.

I tried to remember the previous evening—not easy since they tended to be similar to each other. Not too bad. I hadn't drunk too much wine or gone to sleep too late—it was before midnight. So I'd slept some reasonable, "human" number of hours—even if the hour was now outlandishly early for most humans.

Connie…she'd emailed me at about eight o'clock, my time, to say she was going to a meeting and would be in touch "tomorrow"—she'd put "tomorrow" in quotes to say it would be tomorrow for me.

Even before turning on the computer, I went to the living room window.

Open on the night. I stood there in a T-shirt, pajama pants, and slippers. Cool and lovely, the air fraught with pine scent. Stars over French Hill. A deep *d'mama*—a Hebrew word for "stillness." As if there had never been a war, as if no one had ever had trouble. Pure calm.

When I turned on the computer, there was an email from Connie from ten minutes ago: "Steve, you there by any chance?"

It was unusual at such an hour; she always tried to get me on a more normal schedule, didn't want to encourage me to keep strange hours by making me think emails would be arriving during them.

S-Sandor: Yes.

ConnieLn: You're there? Haven't stayed up all night I hope.

S-Sandor: No, I got up a few minutes ago. I slept OK.

ConnieLn: Steve…not good.

S-Sandor: What's happening?

ConnieLn: It's too quiet here.

S-Sandor: He call?

ConnieLn: No, of course not.

S-Sandor: How long has he been gone now?

ConnieLn: Almost two weeks.

S-Sandor: No good.

ConnieLn: Steve. No sister, no brother, no mother, no father. My fate. Don't know why.

S-Sandor: Connie, it's a lousy fate. It's lousy.

ConnieLn: I would tell myself…but I have a son. At least I have a son.

S-Sandor: You have a son, Connie.

ConnieLn: Moved out almost two weeks ago. He told me—and Pat—not to call him. He doesn't want us calling him while he's mixed up in something, which he usually is. Said he'd call us. He called—both of us, within the same five minutes—once, last week. To me he said, Mom, how ya doin'. I'm doin' fine. That's it. That was really the whole thing. I don't even know where he is now.

S-Sandor: Connie, what can we do. He's still very young.

ConnieLn: Too quiet here.

S-Sandor: I'm here.

ConnieLn: I know. It feels like the one gift I was given.

S-Sandor: Benny is a gift too. He's just in a bad period. A lot can change.

ConnieLn: I'm too worried for optimism. I'm too worried.

S-Sandor: Connie, you have to get away from there already. Even for a short time. Away from there.

ConnieLn: It would be good, wouldn't it?

S-Sandor: Connie. Jerusalem is a real place. The Sea of Galilee is a real place. It has a gorgeous, unique blue color I can't even describe.

ConnieLn: I'm afraid.

S-Sandor: Connie, you need it now.

ConnieLn: I know.

S-Sandor: You going to avoid the whole Holy Land because I'm here?

ConnieLn: It's crazy, right?

S-Sandor: Yes.

ConnieLn: So, it's crazy.

S-Sandor: Connie, do you remember the first night we were together? The first time we went to the pond?

ConnieLn: You're asking me if I remember that?

S-Sandor: It was right around this time of year—late July I believe.

ConnieLn: Yes. I have the exact date because I kept that diary. I'll check later.

S-Sandor: It was beautiful there.

ConnieLn: Beautiful…beautiful isn't the word…. He leads me beside the still waters. He restores my soul.

ConnieLn: You restored my soul that night, Steve. And the next morning…I got afraid again.

S-Sandor: And what does it say there about fear, Connie?

ConnieLn: I will fear no evil, for thou art with me.

S-Sandor. I'm with you, Connie. From someone who's reached the age I've reached, who feels there's no life without you, you have nothing to fear.

ConnieLn: Yes, nothing to fear, if you're sane.

S-Sandor: Connie, we're always there, at the pond. We've always been there since that night. It's why nothing else works for us. We have no place else to go.

ConnieLn: Steve, only you think of things like this.

S-Sandor: Connie, we're there right now. I'm beside the pond, beside the water. You're a few feet away, with your back turned. All you have to do is turn around. And we can have the whole thing again.

ConnieLn: I will not turn around.

S-Sandor: Connie, I swear by my father's bones, I swear by the dust of Louis and Greta, that I will never hurt you again.

ConnieLn: Steve. I can't. I won't. Stop.

S-Sandor: No, Connie, I won't stop.

About the Author

David was born to Austrian Jewish immigrants in New York City in 1954. When he was four his family moved north to upstate New York, in the Capital Region, and David grew up there in an area where there was still farmland with pastoral vistas. Among his favorite activities were writing stories, mostly Westerns; playing a beloved game, basketball; and listening to music, ranging from classical to rock. But it took him until age seventeen to start becoming a pretty good self-taught pianist.

In 1978 David received an MA in English from Binghamton University. After that, already with a small family to support, he worked in Connecticut and then back in upstate New York as an English instructor, freelance writer, and freelance editor, while starting to build up a corpus of short stories. In 1984 he and his family made the big move to Israel—specifically, Jerusalem.

There David worked as English-publications editor at a research institute, but with many of the manuscripts arriving in Hebrew, and with his Hebrew improving, he began to try his hand at translating. Meanwhile—still in pre-Internet days—he was often publishing articles and book reviews in Israeli and American Jewish newspapers and magazines, and still finding time to write short stories that he began publishing in literary journals. And somehow amid all that he kept making progress on the piano, too.

Today David lives in the southern town of Beersheva, and his three grown kids live a little to the north and west in Tel Aviv. David is now a freelancer running a three-ring circus of writing, translating, and editing, and has by now published hundreds of articles, mostly about Israel, on popular Israeli and American sites. In recent years, though, he's put the emphasis back on his first love—writing fiction. That involves drawing on his various experiences and memories from America and Israel while, of course, adding a touch of imagination.

David's book *Choosing Life in Israel*, a selection of his articles, was published in 2013, and his novel *You Don't Know What Love Is* was published early in 2018. He is now a fixture at a Beersheva café, where he still uses archaic tools—pen and paper—to produce initial drafts of the fictional works he finds it so exhilarating to write.